M000195252

COMANCHE WINTER AND OTHER STORIES OF THE WEST

VONN MCKEE

WOLFPACK
PUBLISHING
— EST 2012 —

COMANCHE WINTER and Other Stories of the West
Vonn McKee

Paperback Edition
© Copyright 2020 (as revised) Vonn McKee

Wolfpack Publishing
6032 Wheat Penny Avenue
Las Vegas, NV 89122

All rights reserved. No part of this book may be reproduced by any means without the prior written consent of the publisher, other than brief quotes for reviews.

Cover design by Wolfpack Publishing

Paperback ISBN 978-1-64734-307-1
eBook ISBN 978-1-64734-685-0

CONTENTS

COMANCHE WINTER AND OTHER STORIES OF THE WEST

For my parents, Rusty and Ann ...
The Cowboy and the Southern Belle

THE SONGBIRD OF SEVILLE

EVERY TUESDAY AROUND THREE IN THE AFTERNOON, DEPUTY Willard Sparks took his position in the middle of Sugar Creek's main street and looked to the east. He might stand and whittle a horse figure or occasionally spit a tobacco stream in the dust. Depending on the length of the vigil, he might exchange a few words with passersby. But he kept one squinted eye trained on the horizon.

When the right moment came, he snapped the pocketknife shut, jamming it and the newly shaped figurine into his pocket. "Stage*coach*! Stage*coach*!" he shouted, his voice inflecting like a circus carny. By the time, the coach rolled into town, the deputy had assumed a disinterested stance at the edge of the street and nodded curtly to the driver as he passed.

Sheriff Merle Lankford knew that Willard looked forward to the ritual as much as a schoolboy does a trip to the candy counter. His deputy made a paltry salary and performed a frequently thankless service. Willard would take a bullet for him and, in fact, had done so on occasion. Lankford figured the man deserved an indulgence now and then, childish as it might seem.

1

On this Tuesday, Willard had been standing sentinel for over two hours. Twice, he ambled back to the jail for a drink of water. Something was definitely amiss. The stagecoach was sometimes delayed by high creek crossings or bad weather but the day was bright and warm and a drought had settled over eastern Colorado. Smaller creeks were diminished to gravel beds.

Willard's shadow stretched long on the street before him by the time he spied the stage topping a rise about a half mile from town. Instead of the usual billowing dust cloud and charging horses, he saw the coach barely creeping closer. The horses took short, careful steps as if they were held back by the driver. A throng of curious townsfolk gathered on the boardwalks, their faces turned eastward.

Willard ran to the nearest saddled horse and jumped astride. "Must be trouble. Better go check on 'em," he shouted over his shoulder and thundered up the street.

A quarter hour passed before he returned, escorting the stagecoach and a very unhappy driver. "Just a busted wheel hub, boss!" Willard reported to the sheriff, who stood outside the jail.

"*Two* busted hubs," the driver corrected and jumped to the ground, red-faced and scowling. "Happened when I crossed a little do-nuthin' creek bed about 10 miles back. Hit a soft spot and the back axle dropped pretty as you please on a rock 'bout the size of a sow hawg. Split both hubs. You'd think the devil hisself put that damn boulder there. And that *ain't* the worst of it." He turned to the passenger door, opening it with such force that it slammed against the stagecoach a few times. He shook his head in disgust and crawled back up to the driver's box to reach the top rack. "Reckon I'd better start unloadin' trunks for *Her Highness*."

At that announcement, a bearded, dark-complected gentleman stepped out of the coach. He smoothed his frock coat and clapped a bowler on his head before turning back to offer his arm, in a theatrical sweep, to the next passenger. By now, the citizens of Sugar Creek had crowded in for a closer look.

The gentleman raised his bearded chin high and announced, "I am Alberto Montesino and it is my distinct pleasure to present the world-renowned soprano, Señorita Rosaline De Caro of Seville, Spain." If he was expecting applause from the townsfolk, he hid his disappointment well.

A slippered foot appeared on the step, surrounded by frothy layers of pale blue silk and crinolines. A gloved hand clasped Señor Montesino's wrist. More layers of silk and lace spilled out of the doorway. A collective "aah" rose from the crowd. The splendid lady who emerged could have been described as girlish except for the dramatic swell of her bosom. She wore no bonnet–her dark hair was swept back into waves caught by silver combs. She was certainly of fine Spanish descent. Her cheekbones were high and her eyes were deep set and nearly black. Unfortunately, her lovely face looked as stormy as the drivers did.

Señorita Rosaline pointed back into the coach and her escort Alberto quickly brought out her parasol, opened it with a "poof," then produced an ornate birdcage which held a very large white bird with a swooping yellow crest.

Alberto looked around for someone he perceived to be of importance. Seeing Lankford's badge, he gave a wide, if insincere, smile. "Good sir, could you direct us to your best hotel?"

Lankford stepped forward and tipped his hat at the lady. "That would be the Drayton. Here, you boys," he nodded at two young men standing nearby, their mouths agape. "Help get their bags down. Take them to the hotel." Alberto didn't seem to notice that Lankford had said "the" hotel.

The boys leapt forward just as a heavy steamer trunk hit the ground. Overhead, the driver was already tipping another one over the edge.

~

"THEY BOUGHT up the whole coach so they could ride alone with no stops. I figured it was gonna be a nice quiet run. Huh! I'd ruther have been haulin' fifteen Apaches than them two. Nuthin' set right with the damn Queen o' Spain." The driver, Lanny Proctor, was still worked up. He was at the bar with Willard at his elbow. "It was too hot. Too dusty. Too rough. Bad for her voice, she says. Alby-erto there kept flappin' his hanky for me to stop so she could walk around and do her breathin' and singin' exercises. Like to never got her inside in the first place—skeered of the horses. By the way, how long before I'm patched up so I can haul them dandies to Denver and git shed of 'em?"

"Smithy says he's got one extry wagon wheel but he'll have to make you another'n," said Willard. "He's tryin' to scrape up some hickory or oak. Not much in the way of hardwoods out here. You know, I seen a piece in the Denver paper last week about that lady comin' to do a show at their new opry house. They said she's called "The Songbird of Seville." In truth, Willard had only *seen* the story. He was secretive about the fact that he'd never been schooled. After glimpsing Rosaline's picture, he had asked Sheriff Lankford to read the article to him.

"Hey, Lanny," Willard asked. "What's the story with that big bird of hers?"

Lanny put his head down on his hands for a moment. "The damn bird. I almost forgot. She's got that thing tied to a long string. Called it a *cawkatoo*. Hugs on it and strokes it like it was a young 'un. When she took her breathin' strolls she let it fly around her head in a big circle. Then it'd come back to her. Strangest damn thing I ever saw."

The saloon was busy for a weeknight and the piano player was pounding merrily on an old upright. Every man who had laid eyes on "The Songbird" was packed into the room giving his own account of her arrival. Each was convinced that she had looked directly, even longingly, at him as she made her elegant way across the street. Some reported a pause and a little wave of her hand before she disappeared into the hotel. No one had understood the flurry of Spanish exchanged between Rosaline and the lackey Alberto. Surely, she was expressing admiration for their quaint little town...and its friendly inhabitants.

"ALBERTO, you incompetent bastard! What kind of idea was that to take the stagecoach to Denver? You should have hired us a private coach." Señorita Rosaline perched on the side of the bed, parasol and birdcage clutched in her arms.

"But it *was* a private coach," Alberto said.

"Not the kind I meant. There were *four* horses! You know how I hate those savage things. The driver, he was a savage too. And that big ugly wagon was like being dragged in an ox cart across the desert."

"What do you know of ox carts, dear girl?" Alberto chided her. The very idea of Rosaline De Caro being borne in a peasant's wagon! She shot him a hateful look but said nothing. "Well, we are only a day's ride from Denver. We could hire saddle horses and...but, of course, you would not..."

The hateful look dissolved into fear. By the lamplight, her eyes were like dark holes rent in a sheet.

"No, no. Only suggesting, my lady. We will wait for the wheels to be repaired. Perhaps only a day...or maybe two."

"I am to stay in this dustbin for two more days?" exclaimed Rosaline, looking around the room. The bird, still encaged, sensed her dismay and began to squawk. "Juliette, my darling," soothed

Rosaline. "We should go outside...to stretch our wings. Where is my wrap, Alberto?"

"In this trunk. No, the other. I'll get it for you." He unlatched the steamer and carefully pulled out a long mink cape. Rosaline turned her back to him. He placed the cape on her shoulders and attached the gold chain clasp at her neck. "You must be careful in the night air, even though it is arid. I will make tea in case you get a chill. Do you...do you want me to accompany you?"

"No, Alberto. Thank you. I am sorry for my tantrum. The tea will be welcome."

"At least take your handbag..."

Rosaline knew what he meant. Alberto insisted that she carry a small-caliber Derringer for those times when she was alone. She accepted the handbag from his outstretched hand, checked the knotted satin ribbon at Juliette's leg and left him.

For the first time all day, Alberto allowed himself a huge sigh. *She was sorry for her tantrum.* She was always sorry. But there would always be another, he was sure. He rubbed his temples and walked downstairs to order a pot of tea.

ROSALINE SLIPPED SOUNDLESSLY through the rear door of the hotel. Years of coming and going through stage doors had given her an unerring ability to find her way to the back doors of buildings, however inconspicuous. She pulled the sleek sable cape closer to her face. She had taken the combs from her hair to let it hang loose. But for the ghostly white bird on her shoulder, she would have been nearly invisible in the dark.

A slender crescent moon hung low in the star-clouded sky. *So many stars!* As her eyes adjusted, she saw the dark jagged outline of the Rockies' Front Range to the west. Rosaline walked along the rear alley of the main street buildings. They were not much less impressive from behind, she thought. She passed the saloon, where the hearty voices of ranchers and farmers mingled in song with a horridly out-of-tune piano. Further ahead, she could see a square patch of light on the ground. Judging from the shadowed bars that crisscrossed it, she took it to be coming from the jail.

A few more steps and Rosaline stopped. She touched her cheek to Juliette's warm feathers. The bird snuggled close. "All right, young lady. You may take a short flight. But don't get any notions of flying off with a nighthawk." She nudged the bird's underbelly.

Juliette spread her milky wings and flew. Rosaline held her end of the satin ribbon out in front of her. Accustomed to the length of ribbon tied to her leg—about twelve feet of it—Juliette fluttered in graceful circles over her mistress's head without attempting to fly beyond her constraint. Eventually, she began banking in a tighter spiral and landed in Rosaline's hands. The Songbird of Seville laughed softly...and even her laughter sounded like music. "Someday, Juliette, we shall fly away together, with no satin ribbons to stop us."

Rosaline was still holding Juliette to her when she heard slow, quiet footsteps approaching from between the buildings. There was nothing to shield her and she was afraid to run. Perhaps the intruder would go back, or pass by. She perched Juliette on one forearm and tucked her underneath the fur cape.

The steps continued closer and closer. Rosaline could scarcely breathe. In the dim moonlight she could make out the figure of a large man as he stepped into the alley. He took a few more steps in her direction and stopped a few yards away, facing her squarely. *He must have seen her!*

The big man took one more step toward her, then another. She could see the firm set of his mouth, his narrowed eyes. To

7

Rosaline's horror, he began to carefully unbutton his pants. *No, no... this is not happening. He knows I cannot outrun him.*

Rosaline stood paralyzed, then remembered Alberto's warning. The Derringer! She cautiously slipped her free hand into the beaded handbag that hung at her side, thankful that it was under her cape and had no metal clasp. Her trembling fingers found the cool pearl handle of the small gun and she jerked it up, pointing it at the stranger.

Even in the dim moonlight, the silver barrel gleamed enough for him to see it. He jumped forward and grabbed Rosaline's arm. She saw a bright golden flash as the gun went off. Juliette shrieked and flew from her hiding place. Her thrashing wings created a downy cloud of feathers around them.

The stranger paused for a breathless second. His grip on Rosaline's arm relaxed and he fell heavily at her feet.

She was still standing, Derringer in her shaking hand, when the men from the saloon reached her.

She recognized the deputy, Willard, from earlier. He dropped to the stranger's side. When he looked up at her, his face was twisted with something like horror...or confusion. "Miss Rosaline?"

"Oh, is he dead? Thank God! I was so afraid. He was about to...to..." The words would not leave her throat.

"But Miss Rosaline..." Willard said again. "You just shot our sheriff!"

SEÑORITA ROSALINE DE CARO fell from the skies of grace and abject adoration with one gasp from the stupefied men of Sugar Creek. She was an unattainable beauty who had appeared only hours earlier. The man lying on the ground was a friend of many years, not to mention a hell of a lawman.

"Rosaline! Rosaline!" Alberto arrived, breathing hard. He still wore the frock coat but his string tie flapped loose. "What has happened?"

No one answered him. Someone had fetched a lantern and the sequence of events became very clear. He covered his mouth when he saw Sheriff Lankford's still form on the ground. "He was preparing to attack me..." Rosaline said, her voice weak. Alberto took the Derringer and drew her close. She began to cry softly.

"Oh, my dear, dear girl," he said. "You must have been terrified. Do not cry. It tightens the larynx."

Willard still crouched by his boss's side. "Hang on! I think he's breathin'! Hey, is Doc Kirby here?"

"Nope, he's at home," someone said. "He can sleep through a tornado."

"Here, fellas. Help me pick him up and we'll get him over to Doc's. Careful, now! Plug that chest hole with a handkerchief, somebody." Willard helped raise Lankford's shoulders. His eyes met Rosaline's. They seemed to realize at the same time that he had just become the lawman in charge.

He and a burly rancher named Wells lifted Lankford's body with care. As they made their way out of the alley, Willard whispered to the stagecoach driver, "Keep an eye on 'em, Lanny. And every horse and wagon in town."

Lanny nodded. "Oh, I'll be watchin' em, all right."

"WHAT WILL HAPPEN TO ME, Alberto? These animals will never believe me. I am telling you the truth. That man was creeping right up to me and, and... undressing himself! I had to protect myself while I had the chance." Rosaline had not stopped pacing since they had returned to her hotel room. Alberto sat in a chair, looking miserable and very tired.

"We could leave! Alberto, we could leave before morning. The sheriff is not dead so no one would come after us. After all, I have a concert in a few days and I need to prepare..."

"No, no. We cannot just leave. He could die by morning. He could be dead now. Even if he lives, the news would reach Denver and the story would be in the newspaper before Saturday. That would be ruinous!"

Rosaline laid one hand over her forehead. "The newspaper! I had not thought of that. Oh, that would be horrible. Alberto, we must offer these people money to keep quiet. The concert...it would be cancelled. I...my tour...all of it would be gone."

"I do not think they will take a bribe," said Alberto. "But the Denver concert, it is very important. The opera house is hoping to make a good impression back East. That is why they are paying you two thousand dollars."

"I know all of this, Alberto," snapped Rosaline. "I am not an imbecile."

"It is not good for us to argue. We need to cooperate now more than ever. Here, let me pour us some tea and we will put our minds together." Alberto rose and poured from the pot he had brought up from the kitchen earlier. He handed Rosaline one of the tea cups.

"Ecch," she said and set the cup down hard on the table.

"Yes, Rosaline?"

"The tea. It is cold."

Alberto sighed again. "Perhaps we should talk tomorrow. Good night, Rosaline."

~

DOC KIRBY LAID his hand on Merle Lankford's freshly bandaged chest. "A pretty clean shot, thank the Lord. Missed all the valuable parts." Mrs. Kirby washed his surgical tools in a dish pan. She was trooper of a woman and, after twenty years of marriage, was accustomed to being awakened at night by emergencies, large and small.

Lankford was coming up from the ether and opened his eyes just a crack. Willard sat in a chair at the foot of the bed.

"Good evenin,' boss."

Lankford grunted. He blinked a few times and then said, "I don't remember deciding to pay you a visit, Doc."

"You didn't decide to, but it's a good thing you dropped by." Doc Kirby pulled a light blanket over Lankford. "You remember what happened to you?"

"Not really. I don't know. Maybe."

Willard leaned closer. "It would be a good thing if you could try. You wanna tell us why you were in the alley with Miss De Caro with your pants half off?" He did not want to think the worst of his friend but he had to ask the question.

"De Caro? The singer. She was there?" Lankford grew more alert.

"None other."

"All I know is that I went out to take a piss and saw somebody pointing a gun at me."

Willard leaned back in the chair and sighed with relief. "That explains a lot. So, you're not a low-down brute like she said. And she's not a cold-blooded murderer. Well, at least as far as we know."

Lankford looked confused.

"Don't worry, boss," said Willard. "It'll make more sense to you when you get your eyes uncrossed."

A DEEP, cold quiet surrounded Rosaline. She saw the pale curtains, illuminated with moonlight, and Juliette's covered birdcage on the chair. All else was shadowed. She tried to remember how long since she had felt such stillness in a place. Before New York, before London, before...

From the moment the stagecoach had left St. Louis, the last real city on her tour, Rosaline's nerves had felt jangled by the dry harsh countryside and the violent lurches and noises of the coach. And those monstrous horses...she could hardly bring herself to look at them. They tossed their massive heads and rolled their eyes at the sight of Juliette perched on her shoulder. When they shook their harnesses, Rosaline jumped in fright, despite Alberto's constant reassurances.

In her mind, the western landscape itself was a violent thing. Sharp red rocks the size of ships jutted from the parched, cracked earth. Great raw gashes scarred the land, with gravelly excuses for streams trickling through them. The few animals she saw were gaunt and gray.

Rosaline had spent many years enveloped in privilege. The silken dresses, the gushing adulations, the waves of applause...all conjoined into a life of perpetual softness. Alberto protected her from any unpleasantness that arose, but even he was no match for the hard and unpredictable West.

I shot a man. Rosaline sat against the pillows hugging her knees to her chin under the quilts. *I shot a man.*

Surely, he was dead. He had been only a few feet away from her. The fear she had felt in the darkened alley was nothing compared to now. Her soft, sheltered existence had ended with one awful gunshot.

It was nearly daylight when her head tilted back into fitful sleep. Rosaline dreamed in fragmented images of running down a cobbled street in the night, hearing a man's heavy footsteps and breaths behind her. She ran and ran until, finally, the night lifted and she reached a sunny field. Though she could not see his face, she could hear her father singing...his deep happy voice mingling with the high sweet calls of canaries.

~

THE DRAYTON OFFERED a small parlor and dining room for its guests. Alberto was finishing off his steak and eggs. Rosaline picked at her poached egg and biscuit with her fork. They had overheard that the sheriff was alive but knew no details.

Willard stepped into the dining room and spotted them. "Mind if I sit down?" He saw Lanny Proctor in a far corner of the room, drinking coffee. They exchanged nods.

Alberto jumped to his feet. "Of course not, Deputy. Would you care for breakfast?" He heartily shook hands with Willard.

"Nope...I mean no, thank you. Had mine a couple of hours ago." He sat and tossed his hat onto an empty table nearby. "Mornin', Miss Rosaline." She acknowledged him with a tight smile. At that moment, Willard thought she looked more like a scared kid than a world-famous opera singer.

"We heard that the sheriff survived," Alberto said. "The Señorita...she is very distressed over the incident. It was most traumatic for her."

Willard knew when he was being felt out. Resisting the urge to keep them hanging in suspense, he said, "There won't be any charges. The sheriff was, um, takin' care of some personal business in the alley and didn't count on runnin' into anybody."

Alberto brought his hands together in a prayerful pose. "Oh, thank God in His mercy. I had hoped there would be a clear explanation."

Willard watched Rosaline's face. She was stunned, and after the meaning of his words dawned on her, she blushed deeply.

"The bullet lodged on a rib and Doc Kirby dug it out. The sheriff's a lucky man. Reckon you're a lucky lady too."

"Ah, Rosaline, that is wonderful news! Now you can stop worrying and begin to rehearse. We must contact the stage driver right away and find out if the wheels are finished." Willard was amused that Alberto was ready to move on to business. Rosaline, however, still sat quietly.

"Perhaps I could visit the sheriff...if he would not mind," she spoke at last.

"I imagine he wouldn't mind at all. I'll drop by and make sure he's presentable." Willard winked at Rosaline and she blushed again.

SHERIFF MERLE LANKFORD, duly warned, had talked Doc Kirby into helping him put on a shirt. The good doctor refused his patient's demand to be seated in a chair but did prop him up with pillows. The preparations sent Lankford into spasms of chest pains. In spite of his best efforts, he was still grimacing when Rosaline stepped into the room. Her emerald green skirts nearly filled the small office, which was really just a closed in lean-to attached to the doctor's house.

Doc Kirby parted with a friendly word of caution. "No dancing or anything foolish, Merle." He gave Rosaline a wary look before he left the room.

"Miss De Caro. We meet again."

She sank into a chair. "Are you...in much pain?"

Lankford managed a smile. "Only when I move. Or breathe. Or blink."

"I am very sorry for the misunderstanding." Rosaline's hands flew to her throat as though reliving the incident. She closed her eyes and shuddered. "I thought...I thought I was in danger. It was so dark and I heard someone coming and then you...oh, I promise to you...it will never happen again."

Lankford would have chuckled if he could. "Well, I would hope not. Look, I know it was an accident. I guess I'll have to start announcing my intentions when I go out at night."

Rosaline smiled. "It was a little comical. Not that you were shot but that I...jumped to a silly conclusion."

"Not silly. This is rough country. Reckon the whole world can be rough."

Rosaline looked thoughtful. "Yes, it can. I remember being afraid to walk home after rehearsals years ago. This was before I had Alberto with me. There were street boys who followed me once...planning to rob me, I am sure. I ran into a butcher's shop and stayed until they were gone."

"And I thought I was in a dangerous line of work," said Lankford.

Rosaline shifted in the small chair. "Well...is there something... I could do to make amends, Sheriff? A donation to your town perhaps? I would not like to have the world think of me as a mad woman who goes about shooting the police." She bit her lip, embarrassed at the selfish admission.

Lankford studied her a moment. "Miss De Caro, I don't think it would serve anybody if this story got out, say, to the newspapers. Especially in Denver."

She dropped her head and murmured, "I would be most grateful, Sheriff Lankford."

"You know, now that I think about it, there is something you could do..."

Rosaline looked up in surprise. "Yes? I would be happy to help. I will tell Alberto to make a bank draft..."

"No, not money. You could...you could sing for us."

"Sing?"

"Well, I guess that would be asking a lot. We're just a little foothills town and you're used to big cities and opera houses. I'm sure you noticed that we don't have one of those..."

Rosaline appeared to consider the idea. "I...I suppose I could. But where?

"Reckon the Flatiron Saloon is about the only place we've got. There is a piano...a sorry excuse for one, I reckon."

"The saloon! I have never sung in such a place." Rosaline stopped herself. "Well, I...I suppose it could be aired out, no? Is there a...a stage?"

"Not exactly," said Lankford. "But there could be. By tomorrow night, maybe?"

Rosaline frowned. "All right. It will have to be a brief performance. I am scheduled to sing from "La Traviata" on Saturday and must conserve my voice. I will speak with Alberto to see if he has suggestions for a few arias."

"Is there any chance you know...?" Lankford said haltingly.

"You have a suggestion? From which opera?"

"Not from an opera. It's just an old song I like. Don't get to hear real music often and I just thought...well, it's called 'Home Sweet Home.'"

Rosaline raised an eyebrow. "You could teach it to me." Her face softened and her thoughts seemed to drift. "Where is home, Sheriff?"

"Before Sugar Creek? Aw, a little farm back in the Arkansas hills. Boy, I sure miss the peach trees. And the flowers. Well, I reckon you think that's funny, a big lunk like me missing peaches and rosebuds."

"No, I do not." Rosaline began fiddling with the lace on her sleeve. "I lived on a little farm as well, far from anywhere. We had beautiful flowers. After I helped in the vegetable garden, I would sit under the pergola and look at the bougainvillea hanging down. My father had a few grapevines, enough for our own wine. We were very poor..." She caught herself. "I have never told anyone this...not even Alberto."

She smoothed the green silk dress over her lap, and fingered a dainty gold bracelet at her wrist. "You see, Sheriff, I never saw Seville until I was sixteen. I had been singing for mass since I was a child and our priest sent a letter to a musician he knew. He arranged for vocal lessons and I left my family. I was broken-hearted at the time and needed to get away..."

Rosaline stood and walked to the small window. Lankford remained silent, letting her talk.

"I loved a boy in my town. We were to marry." Her lip trembled at the memory. "He was...he was thrown from a horse and killed. I saw it happen."

"That's too bad." Lankford didn't know what else to say. There was certainly more misfortune in Rosaline's past than he would have guessed. *And she never found anyone else.*

"I never told my voice teacher anything of my beginnings...my real home. When I was twenty, I began performing in Barcelona, Madrid, then London and Paris, even Vienna. I have been working from New York for the past year. This is my first tour to the west."

"Rosaline..." Lankford hoped she would not mind that he used her given name. "I know things haven't exactly gone well and that you really don't want to be stuck here. But...but I would like you to know that I...I happen to be thankful that chance led you our way."

My way, he was thinking. Lankford watched her dab her eyes with her sleeve.

"You are noble if you can overlook the fact that I almost killed you." She laughed softly.

"Well! I have visited too long," she said, coming back to the present, "and I must practice. I will come later today to discuss the concert and the song. Oh, and Sheriff Lankford...that dreadful piano must be tuned. I insist!" The Songbird flitted out the door, forgetting to say goodbye.

PER SHERIFF LANKFORD'S ORDERS, Willard scared up a carpenter to build a small riser against the back wall of the saloon. Sammy, the piano player, dived into the bowels of the old upright with a handful of wrenches, a small hammer and a pitch pipe borrowed from Alberto. Unfortunately, the sawing and hammering of lumber turned out to be at odds with the piano tuning. After a near fistfight between Sammy and the carpenter, the bartender suggested they switch off working for an hour each in order to keep things peaceful.

Willard dropped by with a bucket of gray paint donated by the mercantile store. Both front and back doors of the saloon were propped open in a pitiful attempt to invite some fresh air into the place. All the town talk was focused on the opera singer's concert. Reverend Roberts, who loved classical music, was heard assuring a group of ladies that the Good Lord would not mind their attendance at such an extraordinary event, provided that the bartender kept his promise to only serve lemonade and soda water.

Alberto threw himself into the preparations. He kept Rosaline sequestered in her hotel room until he could make discreet arrangements for her rehearsals. Reverend Roberts offered the use of his home, which was located far enough from town to keep the locals from eavesdropping.

As Rosaline began performing scales in the parlor with Alberto at the piano, then moved on to a series of intricately trilled warm-up exercises, the reverend stood wide-eyed in the kitchen with his wife. "Oh, oh, Janine! She is a *coloratura*! I just knew it."

By Thursday evening, the Flatiron Saloon looked a great deal better than in its entire history, including the day it opened for business. The carpenter went all out with the stage. It was nearly two feet high with steps built at each side. After painting the new riser and the back wall gray, he scrounged up some more leftover paint and added faux white columns as a backdrop, complete with the suggestion of a climbing rose arbor. The bartender removed all the tables for the night and mopped the wood floor. To accommodate the expected crowd, he borrowed every available chair in Sugar Creek and lined them in arcs facing the stage.

Sammy was satisfied that the piano was tuned to a "T" (a term that Alberto found most confusing) and he also gave the worn finish a good rubbing with lemon oil.

"Come on in here!" Willard slapped the back of every man that walked through the door, and tipped his hat to every lady. "Evenin,' folks. You all look mighty nice. Just find you a seat, except them two at the side is saved." He pointed to a couple of chairs with upside-down whiskey glasses on the seats. He was on the lookout for Sheriff Lankford, who swore he was up to sitting through the performance.

The lemonade and sarsaparilla flowed freely and the townsfolk were chattering among themselves when Rosaline and Alberto entered through the back door, rendering the crowd momentarily

19

speechless. Instead of the lavish lace and silk dresses she had worn previously, Rosaline had chosen an elegant and simple gown of white that skimmed the contours of her petite but curvaceous figure. A wide satin ribbon of scarlet encircled the high waist of the dress. Her hair, in ringlets, was pinned up at the back of her neck. She somehow exuded both girlish innocence and womanly poise.

"Damn," said Willard. He and Sheriff Lankford had just sat down.

"Took the word from my mouth, Willard."

Alberto pressed his way to the piano, expressing fervent greetings as he went. Once he had reached the piano, he said simply and with obvious pride, "Ladies and gentleman...Miss Rosaline De Caro." He sat down on the bench and spread several pages of music before him. Rosaline lifted the hem of her dress slightly and seemed to float up the stage steps, without once looking down. When she reached the center of the riser, she turned slowly, slowly toward her audience. Alberto played a soft introduction and Rosaline's face became dreamy. She took a deep, graceful breath and parted her lips.

Whatever it was that the roomful of listeners expected, it came nowhere close to the ethereal sound they heard next. It arose from nothing...like the first star...and gradually materialized in a clear, sparkling beam of pure heaven sweetness. One lovely note melted into another. The voice was at once beseeching and resigned, tinged with the winsome ache of young love and the soft sorrow of old age. The lyrics of Verdi's *Rigoletto* rolled languid off Rosaline's tongue. *Caro nome che il mio cor.* "The dear name that first made my heart beat."

When the applause came, it was with subdued reverence, so as not to break the spell.

With consummate timing, Rosaline smiled graciously and

launched into the lilting "Swiss Echo Song." Living up to her *coloratura* reputation, she tossed out leaping high notes and running trills as if they were light as daisies. She was a creature born to sing.

Next was the impassioned "Ah! Je Veux Vivre" from *Romeo and Juliet*. Rosaline clenched her fist over her heart and seemed to sing for her very life. Willard leaned over and whispered to Lankford, "I ain't sure what she's sayin' but she sure seems all tore up about it, huh?"

The men and women of Sugar Creek stood and applauded... and cheered...and applauded some more. They knew they had been blessed to hear an angel sing, low-flying as she might be. The clapping lasted for several minutes. Rosaline curtsied numerous times. She called Alberto to the stage and he took many bows. When the applause had died down, Rosaline surprised everyone by speaking. Her voice was remarkably soft, but with a velvet richness.

"Thank you. It has been my honor to perform for you this evening. If you do not mind, I have one more brief song."

"Do you know 'Buffalo Gals?'" someone shouted.

Alberto, ever the smiling professional, answered for her. "We are not familiar with that piece. Our apologies, sir."

Rosaline looked directly at Sheriff Lankford. "I...I only meant to pass through your town en route to Denver but...but, as you are all certainly aware, our coach required repairs, which have been completed. I thank all who have made us feel welcome. Also...I apologize for the...excitement I have caused..."

There was a murmur of laughter. Rosaline smiled and dropped her head in embarrassment for a moment. "I am so thankful that it did not end in tragedy. In fact...well, I would like to sing one last song for...for someone who is already your friend, and now is mine...Sheriff Merle Lankford."

She shook her head at Alberto signaling she would not need accompaniment and he left her side. Every feature of Willard's face asked a silent question of Lankford, who only smiled and winked. Rosaline clasped her hands in front of her waist and sang, more gently than before.

Mid pleasures and palaces though I may roam,
Be it ever so humble, there's no place like home.
A charm from the sky seems to hallow us there
Which, seek through the world, is ne'er met with elsewhere.
Home...home. Sweet, sweet home.
There's no place like home. There's no place like home.

The simple, poignant lyric stirred the heart of every listener. Each had come to this rugged place from somewhere else, from somewhere called "home." A green mountain, a fertile valley, a friendly old town, a wide familiar plain of billowing grasses where family and memories were left behind. Here, the strangers had forged a new home from the dust and rocks. With hard work and persistence, they had made houses and stores and gardens. A new life. In twos and threes, they joined in the singing, until every voice melded in the last chorus.

An exile from home, splendor dazzles in vain.
Oh, give me my lowly thatched cottage again.
The birds singing gaily that come at my call...
Give me them, with that peace of mind, dearer than all.
To thee I'll return, overburdened with care.
The heart's dearest solace will smile on me there.
No more from that cottage again will I roam.
Be it ever so humble, there's no place like home.
Home...home. Sweet, sweet home.
There's no place like home. There's no place like home.

After she laid down the last crystalline note and closed her eyes, it was several seconds before anyone could respond. Iron-jawed cattle ranchers bit their bottom lips. Reverend Roberts could be heard sobbing quietly.

Like a sudden rainstorm, the applause filled the saloon. Rosaline was visibly overwhelmed. Alberto shouted thank you's from the corner of the stage and took her elbow, leading her down the side steps. Lanny Proctor, the surly stagecoach driver, lumbered forward and produced a handful of wildflowers, which he held out bashfully. The Songbird of Seville had succeeded in capturing the hearts of Sugar Creek...to the last man.

THE GUNFIGHTER'S GIFT

THE STRANGER RODE SLOWLY, LIKE HE'D BEEN RIDING FOR A thousand miles. To my eyes, it seemed he just appeared from nothing, a sudden outline against the July afternoon sky. Old Jumper raised up from his sandy spot off the end of the porch and growled deep.

It was my sixteenth birthday. We'd just finished having pound cake, something we only had on special occasions. Ma stood holding three tin cups, still cool from the cider we drank. Daddy eased the front legs of his tipped-back chair to the porch boards. He shaded his eyes and squinted in the direction Jumper's nose was pointing.

When the visitor crossed Chugwater Creek, we could see he was of a thin build and wore a big light-colored Stetson that shaded his face. He rode a stocky pinto. Daddy stood then and folded his arms.

"Who is it, Henry?" Ma said, looking at him, then me. "Can you tell from here? Willie?" Daddy said nothing ... just stood there, frowning. I shrugged.

When the rider passed the row of Ma's hollyhocks at the edge of the yard, Jumper barked and started to run out but Daddy called him back. The man was older than I'd first thought, with a darkened weather-lined face. I remember thinking that, for his age, he rode straight in the saddle.

He eased down off the pinto like every joint in him was sore. Then he walked up within about ten feet of the porch and took off his hat. "Henry. Florence. You're looking well," he said.

I was bumfuzzled. I looked at Daddy and his face was red; his jaws were clenched and working. Ma just looked worried. The hair along Jumper's backbone was standing straight up but he stayed put, watching.

The man came up to the edge of the porch where I stood with my arm around a post. He looked right up at my face, reached into his shirt pocket and pulled out a blue box, kind of long and flat. He held it out to me. I can still picture him with those gray eyes looking into mine. Eyes that looked like they could be mean and hard if need be, but that day they were crinkled at the edges... maybe even a little teared up. I took the box from his hands and read the name written on it in silver..."Borsheim's," and underneath that in smaller letters, "Omaha."

"Happy sixteenth birthday, Wilhelmina," he said, his voice soft and rough at the same time.

Without even looking at Ma to see if it was all right or wondering how he knew my name, I took the top off the box and there was the first string of pearls I had ever seen. They looked like beautiful little full moons, creamy with swirls of pink and yellow and blue in the sunlight.

"I know you don't remember me, Skeeter," he said. "I haven't seen you since...goodness, since..."

"Since she was three years old," Daddy said. He didn't sound very happy to see the man.

The old man turned to Daddy. "Three years old. That's right. You always had a good memory for numbers, Henry."

"I remember a lot of things, not many that were good. So, what brings you here, Pap?"

Pap! I should have known. He was never discussed in our house but I'd seen a photograph of him on my grandma Ellen's bureau. He resembled my daddy, only really young...and smiling. I never saw that picture again after Grandma died. *Had he always called me Skeeter?*

"Aw, I guess I done what I come here for," said Pap. "Wasn't sure I was gonna make it in time. Like to have missed the party, I see."

Daddy snorted. "Oh, you wouldn't miss a party now, would you?" I cringed when he talked with that tone. Pap kind of smiled and looked down at the dust. He nodded his head a little, like he'd been expecting the harsh reply.

"No, son. There was a time...a long time, in fact...I wouldn't have. I know it don't mean anything to you but I done quit all that." He put his hat back on and thumb-hooked his front belt loops. He looked like he had a lot to say but didn't know how to start. Finally, he said, "Well then. I'll just be going."

"You...you got some place you have to be, Pap?" It was Ma. She still held the cup handles on her fingers. Daddy shot her a hard look but she kept her eyes on the man standing in her yard.

"Well, naw. Not really, Florence. But that's all right. I need to get on along. Thank you, though. That's kind of you."

Like Ma, I got my nerve up too. "We got some cake left. I wished you'd have a piece with us," I said.

Daddy looked clammed up like he did sometimes when Ma and I outvoted him on something. "Pap, for goodness sake, you may as well stay the night," said Ma. "It's forty miles down to Cheyenne.

And you don't need to be sleeping on the ground when you got kin right here."

Pap bit his lip, waiting for Daddy to say something, I guess. He just looked at Pap and waved his hand like he wasn't part of the decision.

"I'll stay in the barn. How about that?" said Pap. And he wouldn't hear of anything else, no matter how Ma fussed.

I caught up with him before he led the pinto inside the barn. I held the box from Borsheim's to my chest. "Pap! I just wanted to... well, I wanted to thank you for the necklace. Are they..." I was suddenly embarrassed. "Are they really real pearls?"

Pap grinned at my reddening face. "Yes, ma'am. Every one of 'em is a real pearl, Skeeter. Just like you."

PAP'S NIGHT in the barn turned into weeks. He didn't ask to stay. Ma just kept insisting...and he kept refusing to sleep in the house. We could see that Pap was not in the best of health. Without the big Stetson, he looked kind of frail and bent. Funny how that all changed when he sat on a horse.

He and I took to riding together in the mornings after I'd fed the chickens and finished my other chores. Pap pitched in when he felt up to it, probably even when he didn't. Ma went on along like he had always been a part of the household but Daddy, well, he was another thing. He never had much to say when Pap was around. It made for some quiet meals.

Early one evening after supper, I went outside to feed Jumper the table scraps. Pap had hit the hay, I guess you could say. From inside the house, I heard Ma saying something in her "now listen here" voice although I couldn't understand the words. It wasn't long before Daddy jumped in with both feet and they were having a fine disagreement. I stayed outside where it was safe.

"You weren't there, Florence. You never saw him push my mother around, or box my ears, or trade the hog for a bottle of whiskey. You didn't hear whispering in the school yard that your pa was a hired gun..."

I took off for the hen house before I heard any more. I couldn't imagine old Pap doing any of those things. Well, maybe the gun part. He kept a Colt Equalizer hanging on a peg right by his hay bed and blankets. It sure looked like a serious piece of equipment. But to be mean to Grandma and Daddy...that didn't sound possible.

Chickens have always calmed me down when I was upset. They were already roosted and wondered what I was doing there, no doubt. I stroked the backs of a few hens. Their soft feathers and half-closed eyes did the trick, and I finally stopped shaking enough to go back to the house. Ma and Daddy were on the porch, calling for me.

"YOU KNOW, I never have cared much for a spotted horse."

Pap and I were out riding. The grass was nearly up to our stirrups, tall enough to be cut for hay. I knew I'd be out here helping Daddy in a couple of days at most.

"What've you got against a spotted horse?" Pap said.

I looked his pinto over. "Well...I don't mean to offend. It just seems like the spots take away from the lines of the horse. You can't tell much about his cut with all that going on. Looks to me like you can hide a nice-looking horse under all those spots. Reckon you can hide an ugly one under them too." Just then, I felt like I had spoken a little too much of my mind.

"But I don't mean your horse," I added. "He's a fine one."

Pap laughed. "I ain't offended, Skeeter. Guess that settles it, though."

"Settles what?"

"Reckon I won't be leaving you my horse when I die."

Before I could answer, he dug in the spurs and that pinto took off like a racehorse. I jabbed at my Puck's sides and he jumped forward into a fast gallop but I knew we'd never catch up. When we topped the rise at the far south end of our farm, I could see Pap standing under a cottonwood, loosening the pinto's cinch strap. I got down and did the same for Puck.

I hadn't noticed until then that Pap was wearing his gun belt. The Colt's handle caught the sun. The wood was stained dark and shinier in places like it had been handled...quite a bit.

"You expecting trouble, Pap? Not much out here except coyotes and prairie dogs. The Cheyenne have been quiet of late."

Pap touched the holster and smiled. "Thought we'd drill a few pine cones or something. Never hurt a lass to learn to shoot."

I got a little knot in my stomach. Daddy kept a Winchester hanging on the wall...his "skunk killer," he called it...but I was forbidden to touch it.

He tied off the horses to a thick low-hanging limb of the cottonwood. Then he put his hands on his hips and surveyed the surrounding landscape, eventually nodding in the direction of a clump of twisted pines thirty yards off.

"Left side," he said. "Three of them." I spotted the branch with three cones spread like a chicken foot at the end, bobbing in the wind.

I never even saw Pap pull the gun out of the holster. A loud blast filled the air, followed by a puff of sharp-smelling smoke. Puck reared up a little and tossed his head. The pinto was tugging mouthfuls of grass, like he was used to such goings-on. I could see that the middle pine cone was missing from the branch but the ones on each side were untouched.

While I watched, there were two more loud booms close together and the pine cones vanished one after the other. I looked at Pap and was surprised to see him crouched a little. The Colt was still smoking in his right hand and he held his left arm out to the side and bent at the elbow. His eyes were squinted hard. I'd never seen a real gunfighter in my life but I would have bet my string of pearls I was looking at one right then.

"Pap! You drilled them all right."

Next second he was smiling again, just like nothing had happened. He reloaded the empty chambers. "Why don't you have a go at it?" He held out the Colt. I took it in my hands, thinking it felt a lot heavier than it looked.

"But Daddy never lets me..." Pap ignored me and went on.

"Here...hold it this way, Skeeter. You ain't cradling a hen." He guided my fingers around the grip of the gun and touched my pointer finger. "Keep that one free for the trigger. Now, pull the hammer back with your thumb." I figured out that it took both my thumbs to get the hammer to click.

Pap pointed to a pine about halfway between us and the one he'd shot at. "There's a big clump of cones sticking out at the top. Look right down the barrel and put the sight under them. Then squeeze the trigger."

I tried to do just what he said. Next thing I knew, my ears were ringing from the shot and my arm felt like it was broken. I had no idea what I had hit, if anything. Most likely a piece of Wyoming sky.

Pap's voice sounded muffled. "Not too bad for a first shot. At least you missed the horses. Try it again. Maybe use your other hand too."

I held the Colt at arm's length and wrapped both hands around the grip. The pine cones swayed a little in the breeze but I tried to level the sight under the clump.

"When you get them in your sights, hold your breath just before you pull the trigger," Pap said. "Come on, Skeeter. *Draw a bead on the sumbitch.*"

I blushed hotly. I was not accustomed to such language. Nevertheless, I took a deep breath and focused with all I had on the tip of the gun sight. For just a second, it seemed like there was no sound and nothing else in the world except me and those pine cones. I squeezed on the trigger, slower and steadier this time. The shot did not startle me as before, since I was ready for it.

"That's my girl!" hollered Pap. I lowered the Colt and looked at the top of the pine. I saw only the splintered end of a branch...nary a pine cone.

We raced again on the way home. Pap let me win, I know he did. As the house came into view, I was thinking that there wasn't a happier girl in Chugwater Valley.

"WHAT WAS ALL THE SHOOTING ABOUT?" Daddy was on the porch. He had what my Grandma Ellen used to call "a frown on his face like a wave on the ocean." I felt I should somehow take up for Pap.

"It was me, Daddy. I begged Pap to let me shoot at some pine cones. I even hit one."

"Reckon you forgot all about it not being allowed...handling a gun."

"I know you said I wasn't old enough. I thought maybe since I turned sixteen it would be all right. I'm sorry, Daddy. I should've asked you."

I could tell Pap was about to spill that it was his idea. "Maybe you could come with us next time," I said, hoping to cut Pap off and maybe cool Daddy's temper.

Daddy looked from me to Pap. "I don't have an interest in shooting. And I've a notion there are more useful things you could be doing. Why don't you go inside and help Ma for a bit?"

It worried me to leave them. But I said my *yes sirs* and went in the house. Ma was peeling potatoes for supper.

"Willie! Everything all right? I heard gunshots."

"Pap was showing me how to shoot a pistol." Over the fire hung a small kettle filled with water for the potatoes. I jostled the burning wood with a poker. "Have you ever shot a gun, Ma?" For some reason, I thought of Pap's words *draw a bead on the sumbitch* and it made me smile.

"Oh, no. Of course not. Not very seemly for young ladies, in my opinion." She shrugged. "I guess here in Indian country it might be a good thing to know." It seemed she made the last comment to herself more than me.

Just then, I heard Pap's voice outside, louder than I'd ever heard it. "...just spending time with my granddaughter," he said.

"Well, ain't that a noble thing. It's a damn shame you never thought to do the same with your own son."

Ma and I looked at each other, then she dropped her eyes back to her potato peeling like she was embarrassed at overhearing the quarrel.

Daddy was wound up. "I'll thank you to not teach your gunfighting ways to Willie. Don't reckon she knows how much killing money you and that Colt have made. Hell, you probably don't even know..."

"There's plenty *you* don't know about that, Henry. I never shot any man that didn't need killing. It was done for reward money, not entertainment, and most times there was no gunplay involved. I'm done with it all anyhow."

The men were silent for a minute. Then Pap spoke again, calmer this time. "Henry...I know I was a no-account father to you. I didn't do right by your mother neither. I've lived with that day and night. Not until I lost everything I loved in this world to drinking whiskey did I lay it down...only it was too late. Thought I'd spend my last days with what family I got left. I see now that was a foolish notion. I'll be leaving in the morning, Henry. You were good to let me stay this long."

Pap must have gone to the barn. Daddy stayed on the porch and rolled a cigarette. I could smell the smoke from it. We had potatoes and cornbread for supper, just the three of us.

JUST BEFORE DAWN, a hard summer squall bore down on the farm. I was awakened by the rattle of thunder and a fierce wind whining around the corners of the house. Dust blew in through the door cracks. Then the rain came down in a loud rush and did not let up until midday. The south hay field would have to wait.

I figured that Pap wouldn't go anywhere in that weather but I couldn't be sure until the rain stopped. I walked, almost ran, to the barn, leaping puddles on the way. The sun had come out with a vengeance, and steam rose from the water-soaked ground. Pap was currying the pinto. His stuffed saddlebags lay just inside the barn door.

"Howdy, Skeeter," he said. "That was a toad strangler, eh? Thought the roof was gonna leave me a time or two."

"I kind of like storms," I said, "but Ma doesn't. She gets a lot of knitting done when there's a hard rain."

"Say, Skeeter..." Pap stopped brushing. "I decided I'd...I'd ride down to Cheyenne, maybe on over to the North Platte country, to visit some fellers I used to know. Most of them are old ranchers now. Like to see them all before they start getting hauled off boots first."

"I heard."

Pap looked uncomfortable. "You heard."

"Pap, I heard you and Daddy fussing yesterday. I...I wanted to say I'm sorry. If you hadn't been trying to teach me to shoot, none of this would have happened."

Pap hung the curry comb up on a nail and turned toward me. "Oh, Lord, Skeeter. None of it's your fault. This goes way back to when your daddy was a boy. He's got a right to be sore with me. I wasn't much good to him, or your grandma."

"Well, I think he ought to forgive," I said. "That was a long time ago and things are different now. I don't want you to leave, Pap."

He lifted the Stetson and scratched his head. "Wilhelmina, you are a pearl, just like I said. It was worth everything to get to be with you for a time. But I don't think I ought to stay."

"At least wait a day or two. Chugwater Creek's got to be over the willows from all the rain."

"That's so, I reckon."

"I'll talk to Daddy," I said boldly. Pap didn't answer, just nodded.

But I didn't have to talk to Daddy. He walked in the barn just then. "Creek's way up," he said. "Be foolish to try a crossing. I'd wait a few days." That was all he said.

THE NEXT DAY WAS SUNDAY. I only had one dress I hadn't outgrown and I'd worn it to church the last four times. We would sell hogs in the fall and the money would bring calico for new dresses, maybe even a new pair of lace-up shoes. Fluffing up the limp ruffles on my sleeves, that seemed a long way off. I'd been begging Ma to let me wear my pearl necklace to church but she said it would look proud.

"Please, Ma," I beseeched. "If I don't wear them to church, then where? The town dance is more than two months away. I'm aching to show them to Myra Lundberg."

She threw up her hands. "Oh, all right then, Willie. Go ahead and wear them. But don't be surprised if you get some down-the-nose looks."

I was so happy I war-whooped just like a Cheyenne. Ma helped me with the clasp and, looking at myself in Daddy's shaving mirror, I smoothed my collar under the necklace. *Real pearls.* Myra would be so envious, but in a best friend sort of way.

Looking in the little mirror, it was curious to me how much I had changed of late. My frizzy blonde hair had turned a few shades darker and settled down into waves. My face wasn't round and kiddish anymore. I put my hand on my cheek and felt the smooth flatness of it. When I turned away, I caught Ma staring at me, her eyes soft and a little sad.

"You're a pretty girl, Wilhelmina." I didn't know what I should say.

Daddy drove the buckboard close to the porch and Ma and I climbed on. We squeezed into our places on the seat beside him. The wagon lurched and bounced all the way to church but I did my best to sit tall and elegant like a queen.

MA WAS RIGHT. Valeria Hobart about twisted her head off looking back at me during church. I could tell she was dying to know how I came by a string of pearls. She was pretty enough but her mouth always turned down and her nose wrinkled up like she smelled something sour. Then she whispered something to her mother and Mrs. Hobart looked back with that same look on her face. The resemblance was very strong among the Hobart women.

Myra Lundberg loved the story of Pap riding out of nowhere on my birthday and handing me a jewelry box. She made me tell it to her three more times before I headed home.

When we pulled up to the barn, Pap was laboring over a small fire he'd built in the open yard. He was turning a rabbit on a spit and, from the smell, it was nearly done.

"Sunday dinner's on me today, folks." He grinned as he rubbed butter over the meat.

Ma smiled and joined him, holding her skirts back from the smoke. "I have applesauce to go along with it...and cornbread from last night," she said. I was relieved when Daddy didn't mention anything about hunting on Sunday.

I went inside to help Ma get things on the table. Through the open door, I kept an eye on Daddy. He unhitched the mule and put him in the outside pen to enjoy a little grass and sunshine. Pap was pulling on a rabbit leg to test its tenderness. Daddy joined him at the fire.

They started talking. It didn't appear to be a quarrel, just looked like two menfolk visiting. Daddy held a big skillet under the rabbit while Pap eased it off the spit.

"Willie, set the plates and then go pick a couple of hollyhocks for the table," said Ma. She smoothed a cut linen tablecloth on our rough old pine table and straightened the scalloped corners. It had been a wedding gift and I'd only seen her use it a few times.

I carefully arranged our plates and silverware and hurried out to pick the flowers, almost bumping into Pap. The roasted rabbit was sizzling in the skillet he held. "Whoa there, lassie. You nearly upset my apple cart!" He was in fine spirits.

I broke off two hollyhock stalks covered with fluffy blossoms, the palest pink with purple at the centers. Ma held them out to admire them before she put them in a small crock jar. "Grandma Ellen brought those seeds all the way from east Texas," she said, then looked at Pap quickly. I saw her bite her lip.

"Then we better put them over here by me," said Pap, still smiling. I confess that I teared up when he said that. I so wished Grandma Ellen could have been at our table. Those beautiful hollyhocks would have to take her place.

Daddy said grace. Pap passed out portions of the browned meat. He told us a couple of stories about when Daddy was a kid... the time he climbed a tree and couldn't get down. He had to spend the night up there and all the neighbors showed up to look for him. Then the time Daddy and his cousin Pete decided to whitewash the milk cow. Ma and I laughed and laughed. Even Daddy smiled, more than once. It was the best meal I could remember ever having.

WHEN THE DISHES were washed and the tablecloth was folded and put away, Ma and I decided to rest on the porch before changing out of the Sunday clothes we still wore. Pap appeared at the barn door. He led the pinto, saddled and loaded, as if for a long trip. I felt a knot in my stomach. When he got to the porch, he tied the horse to the post.

"Creek's down a good bit from yesterday," he said. I knew it was so. We had driven along Chugwater Creek on our way to church. "Reckon with some luck I'll be sleeping in Nebraska tonight. Ain't but thirty miles."

"That's about right," said Daddy. I jumped a little. I didn't know how long he'd been standing in the doorway. "Long time 'til sundown this time of year. You oughta make it that far." I wanted to beg Pap to stay but I didn't dare cross Daddy. He didn't seem to be in favor of it.

"Well, I'm going up on the hill to visit a lady before I go," said Pap. He nodded toward our family graveyard between the house and the creek. "Like to come along, Skeeter?" I looked at Daddy to see if he objected but he said nothing.

Ma said, "Hold on, Pap. Take these hollyhocks with you. I've been meaning to take flowers up there."

Pap stepped up on the porch and, much to her surprise, kissed Ma on the cheek. "You are a good, good woman, Florence." She looked flustered and twisted her hands in her apron. Pap and I headed for the graveyard. I carried the jar of flowers. I noticed he had his Colt strapped on.

The little cemetery was surrounded by a row of thick cedars that Daddy had planted back when my twin brothers had died. I had been only six years old. The boys, Matthew and Mark, were tiny from birth and both got pneumonia at about a year old. They died ten days apart. Grandma Ellen joined them in eternal rest when I was twelve. I placed the flowers at her marker.

Pap leaned over and traced her name on the carved wooden headstone. "You had no business marrying the likes of me, Ellen Denby. But I'm thankful to my God above that you did. I knew I wasn't good enough for you. Partly why I left like I did. I was a sorry drunk back then."

He straightened up and wiped sweat from his face. "By the time I decided to act like a man, it was too late." I didn't know if he was talking to me or Grandma Ellen.

"Skeeter..." Pap turned to me and took my hands between his. "I want you to remember what I'm telling you. I was a scoundrel on many counts. But hear me out on this. I made my living as a bounty hunter, bringing in some mighty lowdown characters over the years. Most of 'em I brought in alive. I got paid honest reward money for what I done."

"I believe you, Pap," I said. "I just know you wouldn't have killed anybody out of meanness."

"Well, some would disagree. Listen..." He pulled a slip of paper from his shirt pocket, the same one he'd taken my box of pearls from. Only a month ago? He pressed the paper into my palm and closed my fingers around it.

"Here's the name of a bank in Denver where I keep my account. They have orders from me to send a draft to Henry. Ought to arrive within the month. Skeeter, it's clean money and I want you to make sure your daddy gets it. If he don't want it, then tell him to put it in a bank in your name. It's...it's near twelve thousand dollars."

"But Pap..." I said. "you can't give away all your money."

Pap laughed. "I never said I was giving it all away. I got enough for beans and cigars."

There was a sudden great crash of branches behind us and we turned to see a big sorrel horse burst through the cedars only five yards away. The rider was a heavy man with a bristling beard. The horse charged between Pap and me and, before I could react, the man reached down and grabbed my arm...slinging me up into the saddle in front of him. He pulled the horse hard and it reared to face Pap, who was standing, legs apart, with the Equalizer pointed right at us.

"Well, Dub Denby! Reckon you're surprised to see me again," the big man shouted from behind my head. His meaty arm was wrapped around me, pinning my elbows at my sides. "Didn't know you had company up here. Makes things more interesting, don't you think?" He laughed and I smelled tobacco and sour liquor and a rotten odor that made me feel sick.

"You're here to see me, Sid. Let her go," said Pap. His gray eyes were like stones.

"Ha! That'd be tender-hearted, wouldn't it? You wasn't so obliging to my brother Rolf. You plugged him just about...here." With his free hand, the man named Sid pressed the muzzle of a pistol in the flesh just below my collarbone, and the pearl necklace I'd forgotten to take off.

"Your brother was already holding a gun on me when I drew," answered Pap. "She's unarmed and got no part in this. You and Rolf made your way. You knew it was going to end with a bullet or a jailer's key."

"Reckon you got a purty thick wad for hauling in the Gothard Brothers. Damn shame one of us only brought half price, being dead and all. As for me, they's not many jails that can hold me for long. I been hunting you for six months now. And I get to do the killing this time, Dub."

Sid Gothard slid the barrel up to my temple. "Maybe I'll shoot this little gal too. Might be a fine idea for you to drop that Colt about now." I wanted to signal Pap not to give up his pistol but I didn't dare move. I mouthed "no." Thought maybe I could figure out a way to give him a clear shot at this smelly man behind me.

Pap lowered his gun and bent down to lay it gently on the ground out in front of him. Then he took a step backward. "Now... let her go, Sid."

The next minute passed slow, like a dream. Sid straightened his gun arm all at once and aimed at Pap. I threw all my weight to the side, broke free and tumbled off the horse. I heard a shot and got to my hands and knees to see Pap crouched like he was that day under the cottonwood. But there was no gun in his hand. He looked right at me real calm, then he collapsed.

I scrambled for the Colt...still on the ground between us. I must have spooked the horse because he threw his head up and danced backward a few steps...just long enough for me to get my hands on the grip. I knew Sid would be aiming for me next time. When I swung the pistol around, I saw that it was true.

Hold your breath...squeeze! I heard the shot, but somehow, I knew it had come a split second before I pulled the trigger. Was I hit?

Sid Gothard had a quick look of surprise on his face, then he tilted to one side and slid, falling heavily to the ground.

I heard a footstep. *Pap?* I spun around, the Colt still clasped in both my hands. In the gap of the cedars that Sid had ridden through, stood Daddy...holding his Winchester rifle, a curl of smoke rising from the barrel.

We both ran to Pap. He was bleeding from his upper chest, near the very spot Sid had threatened to shoot me. "Daddy, do something for him!" I was on the edge of crying. He leaned over and listened to Pap's chest. Then he stripped off his own shirt, rolled it into a ball and pressed it on the wound.

I saw Pap wince a little. "He's alive!"

"Let's get his head up. Here...can you move around and let him rest on your lap?" Ma ran into the graveyard. Her cheeks were bright red and her hair combs were slipping out.

"Oh, my dear Lord!" she said. "Henry, Willie...are you hurt? Pap? Oh, good heavens, he's shot!"

"We're both fine, Florence. Pap has taken a bullet...and that fellow over there probably took two." Pap moved his hand to his chest, then opened his eyes. He appeared to be in dreadful pain.

"Henry...Florence. He..." Pap whispered.

"Don't try to talk, Pap," I said. He put his hand on my arm, leaving a smear of blood.

"I...never meant for trouble...to follow me here," he said. "For-give me..."

"Don't worry over that," said Ma. "He said he was your old

41

business partner. I told him you were up here. I am so very sorry, Pap. I should have..." Her voice quivered as she stroked his cheek.

"There was something about him didn't look right," said Daddy. I felt a rush of gratefulness toward him. *What if he hadn't come when he did?*

"Henry...I might not..." Pap was struggling to speak. "I need... to tell you..."

"Hush, hush..." Ma whispered. "Can we try to get him to the house?" Daddy was inspecting the entry wound and reached behind the shoulder, feeling for something with his fingers. He nodded. I was relieved that, if Pap was going to die, it wouldn't be there in the graveyard.

The old man would not give up on talking. "Henry...all for you...all these years...saved up. There's money. Skeeter knows where..." *The paper!* I must have dropped it when Sid grabbed me. Without getting up, I made a quick look around and finally spied the crumpled slip resting near Grandma Ellen's grave.

"Hang on, Pap," said Daddy. "Don't get in a hurry to cash in your chips. You ain't going anywhere...least not today. Looks like your biggest gripe is gonna be a bum shoulder." Daddy gently picked him up and I realized how slight the old man was. "Grab hold of that horse, Willie," he called back to me. "We'll figure out what to do with that dung heap later." I reckoned he meant Sid Gothard.

As we walked down the hill...Daddy carrying Pap with the Colt laid on his belly, me leading the sorrel and Ma toting the Winchester...Pap looked up at Daddy and said, "That was a fine shot, Henry."

Daddy grinned, more light-hearted than I'd seen him in years. "Well, I just drew a bead on the sumbitch...just like you told me, Pap."

A STONY GRAVE

Something with soft tickly legs skittered across Marcus Lovell's cheek, waking him from deep sleep. When he tried batting it off with his hand, his arm refused to move. In fact, none of his limbs would budge. He felt a crushing weight from all sides that made it difficult to breathe. A gritty mineral taste filled his mouth. *Dirt?* He blinked his eyes several times. The blackness was so heavy he could feel it. And he was cold...to the bone cold. *Where the hell am I? Why can't I move or see?*

Marcus tried to wiggle his fingers. It was like they wanted to obey but were surrounded by hardness and sharp edges that bit into all parts of his body. He pressed his thumb against the surface. *Rock.* He was buried under rock!

His brain raced in wild search for a memory. *Horse spooked...*

Marcus could barely hold on to the thought. He was groggy and wanted to sink into the shroud of darkness around him. *No, no. Don't let go. Breathing...not dead...*

If he could breathe, then there was space between the rocks. It was hard to take comfort in that, to stay calm. He could smell something familiar. Sweat, rain...his hat! Someone had placed his beat-up bowler over his face.

He attempted to turn, to roll, to sit up, but the weight was too much for his weakened frame. He tried to kick with his boots—left, then right, then left. After a few tries, he heard a grating sound at his feet and felt the stones yield an inch.

Small stones, not boulders. That's good.

Marcus steeled himself for one more strong kick and thrust the heel of his left boot out, nudging the stones by a few more inches. He found he could flex his foot a little. Over and over, he pushed with the left leg until the rock rolled away. By twisting his ankle, he was able to dislodge more stones from the pile. At last, his leg was free halfway to his knee.

Marcus switched to the right leg and began the process again. *Kick and push, kick and push. Stop...breathe.* With the left foot, he worked at pushing the loosened rocks out of the way.

A searing pain erupted within his chest, fanning out to his shoulders. *Damned heart. Don't start with this...not now!* More and more these days, the spells came whenever he was startled or overexerted. He tried to relax, taking slow breaths, but the stabbing cramps made him groan. The pains peaked and began to recede slightly. Within a couple of minutes, the stabs became twinges, then flattened out to nothing.

Take it easy, old man. You ain't runnin' a foot race.

It was Susie's voice he heard. She'd been gone two summers now...died right after Joseph went to college in Virginia.

If I'm old, then I reckon you are too, he used to tell her...just before she popped him with a feed sack dish towel. *Aw, Susie, I could use a little help. See if you can pull a few strings for me up there, will you, darlin'?*

Marcus worked methodically, pushing stone after stone away from him with his boots. When he could finally wiggle his knees, he pushed upward with them until he heard a few rocks topple from the pile. *There you go, Susie. That's my girl.*

From there, he kept at it until his hips and hands were exposed. When his chest tightened with pain, he stopped to rest. He had no idea how much time passed before he rolled the last of the rocks away from his face and could ease into a sitting position. He put his hat on and sucked in a few long slow breaths of chilled desert air.

Marcus rubbed his arms and legs to get a little circulation going before trying to stand. Early September in this country meant clear cold nights and baking hot days. His big overcoat would feel good about now. It was strapped neatly behind his saddle...on a horse that was nowhere in sight.

What the hell happened? And who buried me?

Marcus took his time getting to his feet, then dusted off his clothes. The sky was a deep-into-night violet and the scrap of a new moon was nearly lost in the host of stars. A shattered memory flickered...flimsy at first, like a mirage. The fragmented images took on weight and joined at the edges. He focused hard. *Left the trail...stopped at the new station by Dragoon Springs. All done but the roof.*

He pictured the laborers and the foreman who worked for Overland Mail. *St. Something. St. James...no, St. John. Nice young fellow. Offered me a meal.*

There were four Overland men altogether, and three Mexicans. The new station for the Butterfield line would be ready within the month, they said.

Rode south all afternoon...then through a gap in the boulders. Ah! Helluva rattler coiled up on rock two feet from my shoulder, shaking that tail...

His gelding, Rayo, heard it too. He squealed and bolted through the gap, stumbling on the gravelly path and sliding down the slight incline. They both landed in a twisting heap. Ten feet behind them, the snake vanished into a crevice.

After the shock of seeing the rattler so close and taking such a tumble, Marcus had sensed the attack coming even before he felt his insides ripping apart. He'd blacked out, he guessed. All day and into the night?

The memory slipped away, leaving his brain tired from piecing together the events. He could make out the black forms of scrubby mesquite all around and, behind him, the jagged dark line of the Dragoon Mountains.

The river. Listen for the river, Marcus.

Susie again. Would the woman never stop talking to him? He laughed softly, then rubbed at his temples. God, how he missed her.

All right, Susie girl. I'm listening for the river.

He took a few careful steps, keeping the mountains at his back. The desert floor was pale by starlight but, with his current stretch of luck, he'd probably stumble face first into a cholla patch.

Somewhere out there, the San Pedro meandered northward, from its cradle in the Sierra Manzanal toward the Gila River. It would be higher than usual, at the end of the monsoon season. Maybe he'd get there by daylight. Thirty miles beyond the river was his hardscrabble ranch, cobbled together from adobe bricks and stray cattle left behind by those run off by the Apaches, or worse.

Marcus flipped up his shirt collar and stuck his hands in his pockets. *Keep walking until my boots are wet...right, Susie?*

AFTER DAWN BROKE over the Dragoons, Marcus could finally walk at a normal pace. Normal for a tired old rancher at least.

Long fingery shadows of saguaro pointed the way. Even through the bracing air, the sun warmed his back and encouraged him along.

A broken row of cottonwoods appeared ahead. Marcus stopped to listen and, sure enough, the low murmur of the San Pedro reached his ears. A tiny plume of smoke spiraled upward through the tree branches, signaling a campfire. *Gettin' to be a crowded place around here.*

He moved stealthily, keeping mesquite clumps between him and whoever was brewing coffee at the river. Never had Marcus smelled anything so inviting.

At the feet of a contorted old cottonwood, a young man ministered over a small fire. He poured steaming coffee into a tin cup. Nearby, two horses grazed on the thick riverbank grass. One of them looked very familiar.

Marcus stepped from behind the mesquite cover, about twenty yards from the man. "Hello, friend!"

The young man leapt to his feet, sloshing coffee. When he saw Marcus, his mouth fell agape and a look of pure terror washed over his face. He took a step backward and the tin cup dropped from his fingers.

He's kindly spooky, ain't he, Susie?

Marcus smiled and assumed what he thought to be a nonthreatening stance, turning his palms up and relaxing his knees. The man remained motionless, his eyes wide and unblinking. Finally, his lower jaw worked as if to speak, but no sound came out.

"I'm, uh...just a wore out old traveler," said Marcus. "Don't reckon you'd have an extra sip of that coffee, would you now?"

The man shook his head. "You! Why, I...I buried you yesterday! You're dead! What...what do you want with me?"

Marcus crossed his arms.

"So, you're the fellow I can thank for burying me under a ton of rock. Well, it felt like a ton."

"You were stone cold and white! Not breathing that I could tell."

"It was an honest enough oversight, I reckon. My damn heart tries to quit beating now and then." Marcus took a step forward. "Mind if I warm up by your fire? I'm...well, I'm cold as death." He could not resist the joke.

The young man found no humor in the remark but did relax. Some color returned to his complexion.

"There is coffee. I was about to start some biscuits."

"Don't mind helping out. I ain't the best cook but I was married to one. Watched her make biscuits for thirty-two years."

Marcus walked closer and stuck out his right hand. "Sorry about the scare. I'm Marcus Lovell. Run a little ranch called the Three L this side of Tubac."

The young man still looked skeptical but met the handshake anyway. "Clyde Bell. I'm headed for Tubac myself. I'm newly employed by the Salero Mining Company as a surveyor."

"Then you're used to being out in open country."

"I am, at that. I've spent the last few years on railroad surveys in south Texas. Not much to look at there. This country, however...it's unlike anything I could have imagined. I've seen a few saguaro...they are magnificent!"

Marcus rinsed his hands at the edge of the river. "Got biscuit makings I can start on?"

Clyde pointed to a saddlebag on the ground. "There's an extra cup for coffee inside as well. And bacon."

"Guess I've got used to looking at the cactus here. They would look curious to a newcomer, especially after being in Texas. You'll see more and more saguaro as you head west. And that ain't the only thing different here. We got bad Apache trouble. You're in rough country now, Clyde Bell, and not a good spot to be traveling alone if you don't know the land."

Clyde nodded. "I'd been told as much. I am armed but I can't say that I've slept well. I would probably be in Tubac by now if I hadn't spent so much time looking over my shoulder. My horse has been getting impatient. Oh! Your horse...I brought it along since, well..."

"It didn't look like I'd be needing him," finished Marcus.

"Yes. You really fooled me. I mean, I am no doctor but you appeared to be a goner. Now that I think of it, your limbs were not stiff. I assumed you had only recently...er, expired. However did you get yourself..."

"Unburied? It took some doing. I'm grateful you left my boots on. And I can't say for sure but I might have had some unseen help."

Clyde did not press for a further explanation. The men prepared and ate their biscuits with bacon and drained the coffee pot.

"It'd make sense for us to ride as far as the Three L together," said Marcus. "Not that we're any match for a gang of Apache but at least we'd have company while we're getting massacred."

Clyde packed the cooking gear back into the saddlebag and fastened the buckle.

"That is a practical plan."

Marcus had about given up on Clyde's sense of humor. It was only after they had cleaned up the campsite, saddled the horses and headed westward that Clyde surprised him.

"I hardly think that two dead men constitute a massacre," he said, looking straight ahead.

As they rode, Marcus did a quick check of his gear, trying to appear casual. His Sharps carbine was still in its scabbard. He'd buckled on his cartridge belt, which he had found strapped to the saddle when they left camp.

"I didn't take anything," said Clyde. "I was unsure of what to do with the horse and rifle. It seemed foolish to leave them behind."

"Oh, I never took you for a thief, Clyde, although you wouldn't be the first to take a liking to old Rayo here. Just making sure everything's where it ought to be...just in case."

"In case we meet Apaches."

"They are always a threat, sorry to say. They drove out or killed most all the Spanish land grant ranchers' years ago, then proceeded to eat up the cattle left behind. There are still some small herds wandering the Santa Cruz Valley. That's where crazy fools like me come in. Fine grazing land and livestock there for the taking...if you can keep your scalp on."

"How long have you been ranching here?"

"I brought my wife and son here from Kansas four years ago. Funny, we left because of all the meanness going on there. That was poor thinking, trading bloodthirsty raiders for bloodthirsty Indians. But we managed. We bought a couple thousand acres and have done all right supplying cattle to the mining operations. Well enough to send my boy to school back east. Lost my Susie a while back so it's just me and a couple of hands running the place."

"Have you come under attack?"

"Only had only a few scares. Dumb luck, maybe. Fact is, I feel a whole lot safer at the Three L than I do riding through these hills. I've been up by Mesilla visiting an old pard. Came back on the emigrant trail. Saw a storm gathering ahead when I got to Dragoon Springs and detoured south to miss it."

Clyde was quiet for the next hour. Marcus noticed that he

frequently scanned their surroundings. He also noticed that Clyde kept one hand resting on the Hawken rifle at his side.

"Shoot anybody with that rifle yet?" said Marcus.

Clyde's uneasy expression relaxed. "No. I started carrying it in Texas for the javelina. You may be surprised to learn that I'm a fair shot...for a surveyor."

"I have no doubt. Let's hope all our target shooting is directed at wild pigs and coyotes."

They stopped midmorning at the ruins of an adobe structure located on a mesquite-studded swale. Only a couple of time-softened walls remained, one with a low door opening, but it was enough to provide a slant of shade.

"Could be an old cabin, or what's left of a mission. Hard to say," said Marcus. "Old Father Kino left behind a string of missions back when he was trying to recruit Indians for the Catholic church. Can't say as he did much good."

Marcus was about to dismount when he heard the approach of horses.

"Who's that?" Clyde reined his horse back so he was behind the walls. Marcus did the same but leaned forward, peeking through the doorway, for a view of the trail they had just left.

"Don't know. Not Apache. Vaqueros, maybe...three of them. They're less than a quarter mile back."

"What should we do?"

"They're probably passing through, looking for work further west. I'd hate for them to mistake us for ambushers...which is about what we look like, hiding behind this wall."

"What if they are unfriendly vaqueros?" said Clyde.

"Then...then we'll have to get unfriendly right back. Watch me, Clyde. I'll let you know if there's cause for worry."

Marcus urged Rayo out into the open, with Clyde following cautiously. The riders were a hundred yards away and were pushing their horses at a fast canter. Marcus could see foam streaking the necks of the tired animals.

They're in a big hurry, whoever they are," said Marcus. "They haven't seen us just yet. Not paying attention. One of them...looks like he's hurt. Slumped over."

You watch yourself, Marcus Lovell. These three are trouble.

He had never heard Susie's voice so clearly in his head. He eased the Sharps out of the scabbard and held it low and on the offside of his horse. Clyde was already placing a cap in his Hawken.

"I swear, Clyde, those fellas look familiar. They're Mexican, all right. Where have I...? They look like those laborers I saw at the Dragoon Springs station yesterday morning. I'm sure of it. Two big ones are brothers, maybe got some Indian in them. The short one is pure Mex. What the hell are they doing down here? They run off and leave the roofing work to the Overland men?"

Two of the riders saw them and, at once, began slowing their horses. The third man, one of the brothers, swayed in the saddle, unaware. Marcus could see that his horse was being led by one of the other Mexicans, both of whom wore side arms.

"Buenos días," Marcus boomed. The two riding parties were thirty yards apart.

The smaller Mexican touched his sombrero and answered. "Buenos días, señor. You are well?"

"I am well...Mirando. How goes the roofing?"

Mirando's face hardened. He exchanged suspicious looks with his companion. They had not recognized Marcus until then.

Clyde whispered, "Look at their clothing. Is that...?"

"Blood," he answered softly. "Looks like they were on the bad end of a bobcat fight." He smiled broadly, hoping to keep things peaceful.

"They give us...el permiso...uh, yes to leave. Pablo is not well.

He wish to see his family." Mirando was feigning neighborliness as well.

Marcus looked the men over. Pablo had a wound in his left side and his shirt was dark from the bleeding. All three men were spattered with blood but the other two did not appear to be injured. He saw a broad-axe hanging from Pablo's saddle horn.

"We go," said Mirando. "Pablo is not well, I say."

"Pablo is dead," Clyde mumbled, barely moving his lips.

"And I'd say four Overland Mail workers are, as well."

Let them pass, Marcus. Let them pass.

Clyde asked his usual question. "What should we do?"

"Miz Susie says we let 'em go."

"Miz Susie?"

"We're just resting a bit here in the shade," Marcus called out to the riders. "Glad to share a canteen if you have need."

"No, gracias. We move on. Gracias, señor." The three Mexicans rode past them, bunched together. Mirando slapped his heels into his horse's ribs, anxious to be on his way. The horse sprung into a canter, and the other two did the same. The action caused Pablo to flop back in the saddle. He fell over his horse's hindquarters and sprawled on the ground.

His brother, nerves apparently on edge, heard the commotion and twisted around. He grabbed his pistol and began firing at Marcus and Clyde. Mirando wheeled his horse around and began shooting but yelled, "Vamoños! No, Guadalupe, let's go!"

Marcus and Clyde had abandoned their mounts and crouched behind the crumbling adobe wall. Almost simultaneously, the crack of the Sharps and the boom of Clyde's Hawken answered the reports of the pistols.

"Pablo! Pablo! Mi hermano!" wailed Guadalupe. He shot again, over the body of his brother and toward the wall.

"Dejarle! Que está muerto. Leave him...he is dead. Vamoños!" Mirando was still shooting but wanted out of the fight.

A bullet hit the corner of the wall, spraying adobe fragments into Clyde's face. He reddened with anger and leveled the Hawken again, squeezing off a shot at Guadalupe.

Dust swirled around the Mexicans and their terrified horses. Clyde and Marcus fired again, hoping they were hitting their marks. They heard Guadalupe cry out but could not tell if it was from grief or pain. A sudden burst of hoofbeats confirmed that Mirando had prevailed. The Mexicans, except for Pablo, were gone.

"I think I hit one of them," said Clyde, standing up to watch them disappear over a hillock. He was breathless from adrenaline. "That was...that was awful! Awful, but incredible."

He looked down at Marcus, who sat with his back to the wall, still clutching the Sharps.

"Marcus? Are you all right?"

Marcus was pale and taking shallow breaths.

"You're hit!"

Rolling his head side to side, Marcus murmured, "No...not hit. Just weak."

Clyde bolted for his horse and grabbed a canteen.

"Drink." He dribbled water onto Marcus's lips, then poured some in his own hand and began wetting Marcus's face.

"Come around now. I don't fancy having to bury you again!"

He got a smile out of Marcus.

"Be all right. Just...rest a bit. Clyde, you know, you're..."

"What is it? I'm...what?" Clyde leaned closer to hear.

"You're turning into...a right funny fella."

Clyde sat back on his heels, looking pensive.

"I am, at that."

Marcus nodded that he was ready to get up and Clyde helped

him to his feet, then packed up the canteen and rifles. Marcus refused help getting on his horse. Within a few minutes, they were riding from the adobe ruins. When they passed Pablo's corpse, Clyde said, "What about him?"

Marcus didn't even glance at the body. "Don't fret. The wolves will take care of him."

~

MARCUS WIRED the gate shut on thirty bawling calves. They pressed against the rails of the weaning pen, noses reaching for their mothers on the other side of the fence.

"Aw, simmer down. You children might as well get used to eating salt grass like the big boys and girls."

He checked the water trough and walked toward his house, a conglomeration of planked siding and adobe. A rider approached, waving an arm in salute. Marcus shaded his eyes until he could see the face.

"Well, howdy, Mr. Clyde Bell. How goes the surveying?"

Clyde smiled and dismounted. "It's going well. I can't believe the pleasant weather here, especially considering that it's October!"

"Yep, at least the weather's hospitable. Come in outa the sun and sit. I think I owe you a pot of coffee."

Marcus got the coffee going and the men sat in the small parlor on blue upholstered chairs.

"A nice room," Clyde commented.

"Well, I bought the chairs, and a few other things, to make it up to Susie...you know, for dragging her into the desert."

"Susie? Oh, you mentioned her on our trip. She had said something to you?"

"I probably did mention her. Dang woman is an eternal nag,

even from the great beyond. So, what's the news? I've heard nothing but calves bawling all week."

"Well, you were correct, I'm afraid, in accusing those Mexicans of attacking the Overland agents. The very night after your visit there, they armed themselves with axes and sledges and bludgeoned three of the poor men to death. They cut off the arm of the foreman, Silas St. John, but not until he'd put a bullet in Pablo. Incredibly, St. John survived, but told a harrowing tale of fighting off coyotes and vultures for days."

"You don't say! I had a bad feeling about those skunks. Reckon they're deep into Mexico...probably crossed at La Noria."

"I doubt they'll be heard from again. I can only hope I left a slug in one of them."

They talked further of the progress at Salero Mining and local gossip from surrounding ranches. Clyde stood and stretched. "I should be getting back. I thought I'd take a ride and see how things are with you. If you don't mind, I will stop by now and then. You have a beautiful ranch. And it's good to get away from the mine and have friendly conversation."

"You better be coming by. My two ranch hands ran out of talk a long time ago. And they get sick of listening to me."

They shook hands and Clyde rode off toward Tubac, disappearing into the rolling grassland.

"Well, he's a nice chap, ain't he, Susie?"

Yes, he is. Aren't you glad I sent him your way?

"Well, for Lord's sake, woman. You take credit for everything."

Marcus gathered the coffee cups and put them in a dish pan in the kitchen. He decided to wash them later. He'd worn himself out getting the calves into the pen. The familiar tightness gripped his chest, then subsided. Marcus sat down in one of the blue chairs.

Marcus, my dear. It won't be long...

"Until I'm with you? Is that what you mean, Susie?"

I spoke to Joseph. He'll be all right.

Joseph. Marcus had felt for a while that their son wasn't coming back to the Three L. He would meet a girl, settle in Virginia. That was probably a good thing. Marcus put his boots up on the fancy little table he'd bought for Susie and loosened his shirt collar.

"I hope you're right, darlin', about me joining you. I'm ready to see..."

Hush, Marcus. I'm right here. Do you feel my hand on yours? Now, don't be afraid...

AN ASTONISHING HOST OF CURIOSITIES

CORPORAL THOMAS FOSTER GLANCED AT THE LATE-DAY SUN teasing the tops of the sycamores to the west. He nodded to the soldier riding abreast of him, who then signaled the four cavalrymen to their rear. In unison, the officer and squad heel-jabbed their mounts to a canter. With luck, they'd make it back for evening mess before reporting to the general, who would be pleased they'd found a potential campsite with a clear-running creek and, best of all, an abundance of shade trees. Corporal Foster longed to unbutton the woolen collar of his uniform to cool his neck.

"I've had about enough of this Tennessee dirt in my craw. How about you, sir?" Private Andrew Gillette spit to the side and pulled a kerchief up over his mouth as they rode. "Far as I care, the Rebs can keep this hellhole to themselves."

Foster didn't answer but he secretly agreed. Summer in Michigan and in these godforsaken hills were two very different things. *Pop's probably cleaning a string of perch for supper. That was always my chore.*

"Halloo, Corporal. What's this ahead?" Gillette pointed to a line of what looked like stagecoaches approaching from the south, nearly obscured in a dust haze. Foster raised a hand and reined up.

"Not army wagons, but we'd better stay alert," he said. "Hard to tell how many. Say, have a look at that team in front. And the driver. What the hell?"

They met the enclosed lead coach at a walk, with their side arms drawn.

"Ho there!" Foster motioned for them to stop.

The driver pulled up the team of four striking gray Percherons, who shook their heads and thick necks when they came to a halt. "Hello, gentlemen. Is there trouble?" The bearded man was slim-built with an elegant bearing and curly hair pulled back into a tail. He wore no coat, but Foster noted the unusual cut of his white shirt and the braided suspenders, gold and black. His accent was unusual too. Foster could not place it but guessed it to be European.

Gillette and two other men rode past the big grays to inspect the wagon, leaving Foster and the others to block the road in case the driver decided to take off. Under a fine layer of yellow dust, the coach was dark green with black-spoked wheels and an ornate gold crown painted on the door. Behind it, were three more similar passenger coaches, then several low-roofed wagons, one with heavy bars on the side doors.

While Gillette continued his inspection, Foster kept his Colt revolver trained on the driver. *A traveling show of some kind. These rigs must be stunning when they're cleaned up.*

"What is your business on this road?" said the corporal. "And where are you headed?"

"We are the King and Banks Circus Company," the bearded driver announced, a little louder than Foster thought necessary. "We left Atlanta a week ago and are on our way to Lexington, Kentucky. I am the ringmaster, Count Wilhelm—at your service."

"Count, you say. Can't imagine this is a good time or place to be in the circus business."

"No, sir, these are not the best of times, economically speaking. However, we like to think we bring much-needed gladness and good will during these difficult days."

Meanwhile, Private Gillette had leaned down to peer through the window of the first coach to check for passengers, then nodded to Foster. A shadowy portion of a man's face was visible inside.

"And who's to say you aren't carrying information from one camp to another?" Foster queried the driver. He had heard that sutlers and other traveling businessmen did spy work on the side. "Got any particular loyalties—Count Wilhelm?"

The ringmaster frowned. "I do not. Kentucky is purported to be a neutral state. One of the reasons we are bound there. Of course, we have the utmost respect for the dedication of the Union armies." The ringmaster's smile widened to reveal an even row of very white teeth.

A deep cough—or perhaps a laugh—emanated from inside the coach. Gillette reined his horse closer to the window. "Mind stepping out here, mister?"

A man's face, broad and unsmiling, appeared at the opening. Shielding his eyes from the sunlight, he looked past Gillette and addressed Foster, the senior officer. "I'm very tired, corporal. Is there something I can answer for you, sir?"

Gillette glanced at Foster for direction, who motioned with the Colt to call the passenger outside.

"Seems I detect a Dixie drawl," said Private Gillette. "Where do you hail from? Wouldn't be a Reb butternut, would ya?"

"Oh, he's from Glasgow," Count Wilhelm offered.

"I was talking to *him*." Gillette pointed his own pistol in the direction of the window.

The man did not seem threatened by the gun. "He's right, and so are you—Private," he said. "I'm from Glasgow. Glasgow, Kentucky. Or near there anyway."

"How about getting out of the coach like I asked you?" Gillette snapped.

The latch turned slowly, and the door swung out. The man stuck out his foot, stretched a leg over the coach step and set his boot flat on the ground. *A very large foot*, thought Corporal Foster. The passenger squeezed through the opening, holding to the doorframe for support. *A very large hand, as well!* The coach springs groaned with his weight.

He emerged bent at the waist, then began unfolding and stretching his limbs, seemingly sore from riding in the coach. The man dusted off his pants and straightened up. And up. And up even more. By the time he was done, he stood nearly eye to eye with the mounted Gillette, whose horse took a few skittish steps backward. The soldier stared at the man, taking in the oxen-yoke shoulders and massive head the size of a milk pail. Gillette's eyes met Foster's, then he turned to the giant again, unaware that his lower jaw had gone slack.

From the driver's seat, Count Wilhelm was grinning with delight. "Good sirs, may I introduce to you, The Goliath of Glasgow!"

The grand introduction was met with silence. The huge man shifted uncomfortably on his feet. Foster tugged at his itchy collar. *What do I do now?*

From somewhere beyond the last circus coach came a long and awful trumpet blast. Foster's horse shied, nearly unseating him. *Why, that's the worst trumpet blower I ever...*

Just then, an enormous wrinkled beast stepped from behind the caravan and sounded the horrible blast again.

Gillette swore and instinctively swung his revolver toward the animal. Before he could form the next thought, his entire forearm was enclosed in the gargantuan hand of Goliath.

An elephant! Foster shook his head in disbelief, having only seen such animals on the pages of books. *What the hell?*

THEO MCCULLUM'S farm lay nestled in a hollow that bisected a meandering valley created by Marrowbone Creek. Theo and Betsy sat on an oak bench on the front porch of their cabin. With one finger, Betsy traced the woodgrain of the bench, worn shiny from years of day's-end sitting.

"He said he might be coming home soon," Betsy said, as she had every evening since the receipt of her son's last letter some three weeks before.

"That'd be good." Theo tamped tobacco into his pipe with the handle of a pocket knife. "Been too long." He knew the letter by heart, as Betsy had read it to him several times.

"I worry about him out there." A sad smile softened Betsy's weathered face.

Theo nodded. "Me too." Dusk gathered to the east and a whip-poorwill sang out. Theo listened for an answer to the bird's mournful call, but there was none. He struck a match on his boot sole and lit the pipe. The sweet-smelling smoke tendriled in front of him and the pipe bowl glowed as he inhaled.

"Let's go inside. It's getting dark," she said.

"You sure? It's nice and cool out here. Look—there's the lightning bugs coming out for you."

"Stop trying to cheer me up, old man." Betsy nudged Theo with her elbow. "I'll be alright. Once Stanley ever comes home." She got up and started inside. "Damn war."

"Now, look out, woman. Better mind your tongue." Theo

stayed on the bench, intending to finish his pipe. "Them church ladies find out what a fresh mouth you got, why they'll ..."

Betsy froze at the door and locked eyes with Theo. They both heard the rumble of a wagon on the lane leading from the woods.

"Go on! Get in the house!" Theo sprang up and pushed Betsy into the cabin and slammed the door behind them. By the time he dropped the wooden bolt into place, she had fetched the long rifle. He took it from her and moved next to the front window.

"Is it soldiers? Or is it Aikens? Can you see?" whispered Betsy. She peeked around the corner of the stone fireplace, where she had taken cover. The quavering glow of the fire lit her fearful face.

"Hadn't reached the clearing yet. I don't think it's Aikens's band. They'd be storming in here, hell bent." Theo wished he could be sure of that himself.

Aikens was a Union sympathizer and troublemaker who'd gathered up a dozen like-minded men–Aikens's Avengers, they called themselves. They'd invaded a couple of farms nearby, riding their horses through the crops and, recently, burning a barn belonging to a family with two sons in the Confederate army.

"Go to the back room, Betsy. Let me handle this." Theo peered around the feed sack curtain but already it was too dark to see. He heard the commotion of horses and the squeak of a wagon seat, then heavy footsteps running toward the house. There was the clomp of boots on the porch, then the front door crashed open, splintering the bolt. Theo staggered backward, too startled to take aim.

Betsy ran from the back room and toward the door, her arms up and apron flapping. "Stanley! Oh, my Stanley!" Theo propped the rifle against the wall and they both ran toward the intruder.

"Ma! I'm home! I'm sorry about the door. I didn't know you'd bolt..."

"Oh, don't you worry about the door, sweet boy." Betsy was in tears. "Pa will build another one. Oh, look at you."

Theo and Betsy nearly disappeared as they were wrapped in the giant, Goliath embrace of their son.

BETSY WATCHED Pia and Luisa flit among the rows of corn, deftly plucking ripened ears from the stalks. They had, between them, already picked a bushel of peas. It seemed to Betsy that the trapezists floated through the garden, with their feet barely having need of the ground. After seeing the mother and daughter practice their heart-stopping routines with patriarch Enzo and Pia's twin brother Pasqualé, Betsy decided that the entire clan of Soaring Cavellinis had little use for the earth. They preferred to be aloft—stepping lightly along the tightrope strung between posts in the barn or twirling gracefully on swings through thin air.

Betsy still marveled at the strange collection of people and animals that filled the barn and every available outbuilding. Ring-master Wilhelm had wanted to set up some of the smaller circus tents for lodging, but Theo warned that they should try to stay out of sight—as much as a troupe of circus performers and a few dozen exotic animals can stay out of sight, at least.

Well, after giving birth to a giant, I suppose nothing should surprise me. Betsy held her apron corners like a basket filled with summer's bounty of fat carrots, potatoes, and squash. Maybe little Pia would help peel vegetables for supper. Certainly not Katerina, the trick rider—or *equestrienne*, as she preferred to be called. Although she took fastidious care of her horses, she showed no interest in menial housework.

A fine spray of water rained down on Betsy from behind. She spun around, still holding the apron corners. Mary Ann, the elephant, waggled her ears and opened her mouth in what might have passed for a smile.

"Mary Ann! You little hooligan!" Water dripped from Betsy's hair. "And, you—Jacob. Why, I think you're behind this mischief!"

The animal trainer, Jacob, stifled a grin. "I took Mary Ann to the creek for a bath. When I saw her drinking, I feared she was saving a surprise for you. She has taken a liking to you, Missus McCullum."

"Only because she knows that where I am, there's vittles close by." Betsy worked hard to sound vexed. She couldn't deny she'd grown fond of the big gray beast. "Here—let me set this down." She emptied her apron onto the porch, picked out a large yellow squash, and held it up to the elephant. The squash disappeared into the curl of Mary Ann's trunk.

Betsy shook her head. "I shouldn't be encouraging such rascally behavior. And I suppose we can't have Danté feeling left out. I have some chicken necks in the kitchen. You can take them to him when you go to the barn."

"Thank you, Missus McCullum. You are very kind." Jacob half-bowed to her as she went inside to get chicken parts for Danté. *Feeding the Bengal tiger in my barn. No, nothing surprises me of late.*

"REALLY, the biscuits, Misses McCullum. I have never tasted anything so sublime. Why, they're as light as swan's down, with a crust of heavenly gold."

Wherever it was that Count Wilhelm came from, Betsy figured they must not have heard of mixing up lard, flour, and buttermilk. The ringmaster ate three or four biscuits at every meal, savoring each bite. He never failed to offer up a flowery description, each different than the last.

Theo, along with their son Stanley, went hunting most mornings to provide enough venison, squirrel, and rabbit meat to feed a circus troupe. Jean-Charles—who spent hours training four spotted terriers, three tiny ponies, and a peregrine falcon named Fantôme—had a talent for trapping mice and birds to feed his menagerie. The clowns, Bones and Dino, kept the woodpile stocked and the Cavellinis pitched in wherever they were needed.

Although Betsy never witnessed them in the act, she suspected that the trick riders Katerina and Stefan might be responsible for the baskets of berries and wild plums she often found on the porch. The pair kept to themselves, even sitting apart from the others at mealtime. Betsy wondered if they were brother and sister, or something else. Stanley mentioned, in passing, that Katerina was King and Banks's most popular act. She did several routines with Stefan but, for her finale, she did solo tricks on horseback—her hip-length wavy hair cascading over a skin-colored tight-fitting suit. Betsy noticed the effect she had on most of the men. Even Theo threw a sidelong glance in Katerina's direction now and then.

The most smitten of all was Lord Minikin–all thirty-seven inches of him. His size alone made him a popular spectacle, but he also performed sword and knife-throwing tricks. Even on warm days, Lord Minikin donned a full dress military uniform with medals and a sash. He was solicitous of Katerina, suggesting that she get some rest or asking if she would like a drink of water. She usually ignored him, as she did everyone.

Stanley, the famed Giant of Glasgow, was the gentlest of all the circus personalities, which made Betsy proud. She'd baked an apple sheet cake, his favorite. He carefully cut slices for everyone before serving himself. When dinner was done, he sat on the edge of the porch with his tree-trunk legs stretched out. Theo and Betsy perched on the bench. The performers drifted out to the barn to tend to the animals and other end-of-day chores. Lord Minikin stood in the clearing, smoking a cigar.

"Wilhelm thought we should stay put for a couple more weeks, if it's agreeable to you," said Stanley. "There are troops on the move. Kentucky won't stay neutral much longer, maybe never really was. Yanks are getting more hostile toward anything that looks, talks, or smells southern, even if it's not in a gray uniform. We could slip out when things calm down, maybe take a riverboat back down to New Orleans."

Theo was already puffing on his pipe. "That'd be fine, son. You know you're welcome as long as you'll stay. Friends too."

Betsy could sense there was more that Theo wasn't saying. So, could Stanley.

"Look...I know it was rough on y'all—me being in the army. The *wrong* army, according to most folks around here. But I ..."

"You don't need to make no apologies, Stanley," said Theo. "You done what you felt was right. Comes down to taking care of you and your own. After our McCullum people in Virginia was cut down by Yanks, hell, I wanted to jump in the fight myself. Wished I'd been able to. Hell being old."

"I'd still be in the fight, if it wasn't for my own clumsiness."

Betsy fidgeted. She did not like to dwell on Stanley's injury. She'd cried and hung on to his coat when he joined the Confederate Infantry, cried over every letter he sent—when he wrote of surviving skirmishes, of the dreadful sickness in the camp during the winter, and of the cannonball blast that filled his right side and arm with shrapnel. It's hard to hide a giant on a battlefield.

"Just keep low for a while, son. It'll ease up around here," said Theo.

Stanley studied his father's face, shadowed under a straw hat.

"Pa, I know about Murph Aikens and his bunch. They're too yellow to go off to war so they hide behind a politician's vote of neutrality. Then they raid their neighbors in the name of the Federal Army."

Stanley shook his head slowly, as if remembering. "Aikens wouldn't have made it a week out there. Damn coward. If he finds out I joined the circus, he'll think it was to keep from returning to the front."

"Don't worry about him, Stanley. He don't know about the circus and won't if I can help it. And, yes, I know why you didn't come home after you got hurt. You was afraid Aikens would come around and hurt us trying to get to you. Like you say, he's a coward. He'd ambush a wounded man. So, the circus came along at the right time. You was protecting *us* by staying away, not yourself."

Lord Minikin dropped the stub of the cigar and snuffed it with the toe of his child-sized boot. He nodded a good night to the McCullums and walked stiffly toward his quarters—a stone-lined root cellar dug into a mound behind the cabin.

"No small thing, moving a circus when no one's looking," said Stanley. "Let's pray we find a way to get to the river unnoticed— especially by Murph Aikens."

THEO HAD a whitetail buck in the sights of his old Mississippi rifle when the hoarse bawling of a calf cut through the air. The buck's tail shot up and he disappeared into a thicket before Theo could trigger. Somewhere beyond, the crack of a small caliber pistol rang out and the calf went silent in mid-bawl.

"What the devil?" Theo nearly dropped the gun.

Stanley eased the sling of his own rifle off his shoulder. "We'd best go see. But stay quiet and follow me." Holding the gun close across his chest, he stepped forward and worked carefully through the underbrush with surprising stealth. Theo trailed him, trying not to step on pinecones and sticks.

Their livestock—a half dozen cattle and a few hogs—grazed free in the woods surrounding the cabin. Theo knew there were a couple of cows with calves at side, though he hadn't run across them in several days.

They came to a shallow-running branch, which Stanley crossed with one step. The opposite bank was three feet high and, just beyond, a fallen beech tree lay neatly across the path, providing cover. Stanley and Theo crouched behind it and peered between the dead limbs.

A man squatted beside the dead calf, his back to them. He angled the calf's head backward with one hand and stuck the tip of a ten-inch hunting knife to its throat. His Baby Dragoon lay on the ground a few yards away.

"That'd be a McCullum calf you're laying a blade to," said Stanley, his voice soft, but with the weight and rumble of a millstone. The trespasser whipped his head around and took in the sight of the seven-and-a-half-foot man holding a rifle on him. The knife fell from his hand.

"You're Bennie Cox, ain't you?" Theo called, stepping from behind the tree. Now, the would-be butcher had two rifles trained on him.

The man said nothing. His eyes never left the giant with the gun.

"Yeah, Bennie Cox—cousin to Murph Aikens," said Theo. "You ride with those bastards, don't you? Burning out good folk in the name of—in the name of *nothing*. If you was so all-fired for the Union, reckon you'd join up. But that might be dangerous, mightn't it?"

Stanley walked closer and put a huge foot on the Dragoon. Bennie Cox, still on his haunches, ducked his head and waited for the consequences.

"Give me that," said Stanley, stretching out his left hand.

Bennie swallowed hard and, with a trembling hand, laid the hunting knife in the giant's palm. Stanley tucked his rifle under his arm and gripped the knife handle in one hand. With the other, he proceeded to bend the blade. Like a piece of tin, it curved in his hands until the point was at a right angle to the handle. Stanley handed the ruined weapon back to Bennie.

"Get on out of here," Stanley growled.

"You know they'll be coming." Theo hung strips of beef on hooks in the smokehouse as Stanley handed them to him. "You got to get everybody ready. Slip out before Aikens can get a party up. It's not even noon. You could be gone by ..."

Count Wilhelm appeared at the smokehouse door, smiling broadly. "Veal for supper? What a glorious occasion!"

"Wilhelm ..." Theo said. "We ran into one of Aikens's men today. He saw Stanley. Knows he's staying here. You'll have to leave—for your own hide's sake. Aikens's Avengers, he calls them—they'll be here, maybe as soon as tonight. Can you round up the others? And the animals?"

The smile drained from Count Wilhelm's face. "I see," he said. He stroked his beard, then turned to stare at the barn. He took a few steps in that direction, then looked back, his eyes lingering on Theo.

"Stanley. Meet the rest of the troop in the barn as soon as you're finished so that we may discuss our stratagem. And, Mister McCullum, I hope you'll make good on that veal supper."

Theo smiled wanly. "The missus and me would be honored."

BETSY STARTED PEELING potatoes as soon as she heard. She would get supper ready early, long before sunset, so the King and Banks Circus troupe could get moving. Maybe there was time to bake one last apple sheet cake for Stanley before he was gone.

The Soaring Cavellinis were first in line for the tender veal swimming in brown gravy. Supper was a quiet affair with no conversation, only the sounds of forks and knives scraping on tin plates. Dino and Bones, the clowns, were as somber as undertakers. Betsy walked around the crowded room and porch. *More coffee? More potatoes? Please, one small piece of cake.*

The animal handlers, Jacob and Jean-Charles, sat close to one another, occasionally speaking in whispers and motioning with their hands, apparently working out the fine details of evacuating an elephant, a tiger, a falcon, four dogs, and numerous horses, large and small. Lord Minikin wore his sword and sheathed daggers, in readiness for the journey. For the first time, Katerina and Stefan sat on the hearth near the others, plates balanced on their laps. Count Wilhelm rose from his seat at the kitchen table and kissed Betsy on both cheeks.

"Dear, dear Misses McCullum. You have certainly outdone yourself with this sumptuous meal. The veal cutlet all but melted on my tongue. And, should I never taste another biscuit, your exemplary creations will ever endure in my memory. Certainly, God's own manna from above was not so delectable."

Betsy surprised herself, and Theo, by planting a shy kiss on the ringmaster's cheek. When the meal was finished, the performers carried their dishes to the kitchen and hurried outside without further talk. Betsy took a kettle of hot water from the stove and tipped the spout over the pan of dirty dishes. To her surprise, someone took the handle from her. She looked up into the amber eyes of Katerina.

"Please. Allow me," she said, her pouty lips curved into a fetching smile.

BY THE THIRD time Bennie Cox had told the story of his confrontation in the woods with the giant Stanley McCullum and his trigger-happy pa, the details were heavily embellished. The final account was that the McCullums had called Murph Aikens's Avengers a bunch of no-account cowards and that, in retaliation, Bennie had engaged in a knife fight with Stanley, besting the giant after a long struggle. He produced the bent hunting knife as proof that he would have gutted the big brute if only the blade hadn't struck a belt buckle.

Murph and the rest of the raiders expressed some disbelief that such a thing could occur, but eventually conceded that hand-to-hand combat with giants could have surprising and unexplainable outcomes. Bennie also implied that Stanley and old man McCullum might have threatened the Avengers with a nighttime ambush, which could possibly include the murder of children and desecration of women belonging to the Aikens clan, and any kindred clans as well.

As the corn mash in the jug being passed around dwindled, the level of outrage rose. Murph Aikens, Bennie Cox, and eight other men voted to raid the McCullum farm at nightfall. The remaining four of the Avengers declared their regrets that they would not be able to join the fight against the bloodthirsty giant. It was early August, after all, and there was a pressing need for chopping firewood for winter.

THEO AND BETSY, uneasy after the run-in with Bennie, had decided against sitting on the porch to watch dusk fall. Stanley came to the cabin to bid them good night.

"We are ready," he said, "but we won't move out until morning. Just stay inside—and don't worry."

"Well, I'm sorry you're leaving, son," said Theo. "That Aikens, he's a thorn in the side for everybody around here."

"He won't bother you after I leave."

Theo squinted. "What makes you so sure of that?"

"I don't know," Stanley shrugged. "Just a feeling. I've learned to read a man, I guess."

"Good night, my darling Stanley," said Betsy, reaching up for a hug. "Someday you'll come home to stay. Promise me?"

Stanley bent down to receive his mother's embrace, then crossed his heart with his fingers. "I promise. Rest well."

"WE'LL FIRE off a couple of shots and call Stanley and his pa outside," said Murph Aikens. "Hank and Lon, y'all got the torches. You know what to do with 'em."

The raiders gathered by a creek about two miles from the McCullum farm. Turkey feathers adorned their crumpled hats and hung from their pommels, and every man wore a blue kerchief over his nose and mouth. The fading sunlight slanted gold across the floor of the forest.

"Move out!" Aikens pulled up his mask and motioned with a sawed-off shotgun.

The raiders, riding two abreast, checked their restless horses when they reached the lane leading to the farm. They would hold to a walk until the cabin was in sight. The *skree* of a hawk caused Bennie Cox's sorrel to snort and try to turn aside. The hawk sounded close by. Bennie shaded his eyes and searched the trees. He caught a fleeting shimmer of gray, crossing the lane about fifty yards ahead.

"Murph? You see that?"

Aikens ducked his head to miss a low-hanging hackberry branch. "See what?"

"I saw...I don't know. Something purty big crossed the road."

"Probably a hog or something."

They rode in silence for a few minutes. A few fireflies glowed among the tree trunks and undergrowth. A frog chorus swelled in song. Then, Bennie and Aikens both pulled the reins up hard, nearly causing a pileup of men and horses behind them. Bennie's mouth gaped open. "Whaaaa ...?"

Like a figure from a half-waking dream, a beautiful gray horse, dappled in the evening shadows, stood facing them on the lane ahead. It was large—a draft horse—but unlike any work animal they had seen. Its long mane and pale forelock were the color of corn silk. Delicate silver chains circled each fetlock. In place of a bridle was a scarlet ribbon looped around its nose, trailing back to reins. The horse turned, as if by unseen command.

Murph Aikens gasped and rubbed his eyes, certain they deceived him. A glorious creature lay forward on the horse's back, with her head on its withers and her body draped along its back. Her dark hair billowed in waves, covering her back and falling in locks that grazed her bare legs. From this distance and in the dimming light, she appeared to be wearing nothing at all.

The woman gazed downward, as if unaware of being observed. Her arms encircled the gray's neck. Then, the horse stepped off the road and disappeared into the trees. Without a word, the enraptured raiders touched heels to their mounts and moved forward.

Now and then, they would steal a gray-and-flesh-colored glimpse of the horse and rider. She rode without direction, sometimes appearing to their left or to their right, never moving in a straight line and always ahead, barely in sight. The men rode on through brambles and ravines—following, following like a flock of doomed sheep.

The sky's remaining light shone in lavender shards among the tree branches. The raiders pushed through a tangle of blackberry vines, oblivious to the thorns tearing at their legs, and their horses' as well. Aikens waved at the torch bearers, who rode behind them, to come up alongside. *A naked girl on a silver horse. Could that be so hard to find?* He had almost forgotten the purpose of his mission.

They reached two oaks spaced about twenty feet apart. A sudden shower of yellow sparks sprayed from beside each of the trunks, arcing over them. The horses squealed and twisted, this way and that, a few of them stumbling. Aikens looked left, then right, for the sources of the sparks. He saw two ghastly white faces, one at each side of them, with large, terrifying eyes rimmed in black. The red-rimmed mouths of the creatures were agape, with yellow teeth bared.

The raiders scattered like birds, some cursing and some screaming, all hunkered down as close to their saddle horns as they could get. Aikens was nearly thrown when his horse ran over a rotting log. Finding the stirrups again, he pulled up, searching wildly for his men. He saw torch lights bobbing and weaving ahead, which meant Hank and Lon were ahead, and spurred hard to catch up with them. Behind him, he heard a few horses crashing through the underbrush, they and their riders retreating for home.

"Lon! Wait up!" Aikens hollered. He was almost close enough to touch the flank of Lon's big roan, when a shrill *skreeeee* sounded over his shoulder and a slim hawk plummeted from nowhere, snatching the torch from Lon's grasp and flying ahead in a pale streak.

"It's devils, Murph!" Lon wailed. "We got to get away from here!"

Aikens was about to agree but a flash of dappled gray ahead changed his mind. *The girl!* She sat astride the enormous horse, facing them and holding Lon's torch in her hand. The golden light revealed a lovelier face than he'd even imagined. *Such pale skin. Those dark eyes and full lips—and that hair.* Her dark locks hung to her waist and he could see now that she was clothed, but in a skintight, flesh-colored garment that fit like a stocking. *Had she turned into a hawk and taken the torch?* He dismissed the notion when he saw a falcon perched on her shoulder. The girl smiled slightly and wheeled the gray around with a flick of the scarlet ribbon reins in her other hand.

Maybe Lon was right. Maybe there was evil all around them —and the girl might be a devil herself. Only one way to find out.

Aikens laid spurs to his horse again and gave chase.

BENNIE COX and two of the Nichols brothers split off to the right when the yellow sparks started flying. He thought he'd seen a ghoulish face, white and greasy like wet paint, peeking from the shadows. The creature held a stick that sprayed fire from its tip. There must have been two of the creatures since the sparks came from both sides. A sulfury smell still hung on the air.

The men charged through the woods, trusting their horses to find a path through the darkening forest. They headed for a break in the trees, hoping to find a clearing beyond.

"Bennie! Watch out!"

Bennie's brain hardly had time to register the crisscrossed lines stretched in front of him before he rode straight into them. The lines were woven into a pattern—*a spider web?* He was plucked from his horse by the impact and traveled through the web head-first. He found himself hanging upside down with his foot caught, body dangling several feet off the ground. When he was able to focus, he saw that Jeb Nichols had been snared as well. He was suspended upright, but his forearms were laced between the ropes, making him look like a strung-up squirrel about to be skinned. The younger Nichols brother was nowhere to be seen.

"Jeb! Can you wiggle loose? Can you reach my foot?" Bennie had trouble speaking with the blood pounding in his head. But Jeb wasn't looking at Bennie. Horror washed over his face as his eyes fixed on something in the near distance—something up high.

Bennie heard a *swiiiish* coming from the trees to his right. He was aware only of seeing a dark form flying through the air toward him, then of being grabbed by the ankles and snatched from the rope web. Like a mouse hanging upside down in an owl's grasp, Bennie was carried up, up in an arc, then felt the grasp on his ankles let go. The motion sent him into an upward spin and, as he swung upright, there was another *swiiiish* and a second dark form snagged him by the wrists. When he and his captor reached the end of the arc, they were suspended for a breathless few seconds, then they began a sickening fall in the opposite direction.

Jeb Nichols had been pulled into the game of terror as well. In midair, Bennie's wrists were freed but, this time, he was passed back to the other flyer as Jeb was released. He and Jeb passed within inches of each other, flipping head over heels. Again, they were captured by wrists or ankles and the swinging motion continued, with his body and Jeb's tossed back and forth like rag dolls. Black treetops, purple sky and shadowed ground spun past Bennie's eyes. Just before he lost consciousness, he felt himself swinging slower and not as high as before. His eyes were closed by the time the mysterious flyer laid him down on the grass, ever so gently.

WAYLAND NICHOLS, Jeb's youngest brother, had troubles of his own. After yelling at Bennie to watch out for the rope trap, he'd tried to circle around the contraption so he could help free the men. When the first of the rope swingers whizzed by in front of him, his mare had decided she wanted no part of the game. The startled nag dropped her head and commenced to buck. Once she was shed of her rider, she turned for the long gallop back to the barn.

Wayland had narrowly missed a few trees on his journey and landed just shy of a wagon-sized limestone boulder. It took him a minute to suck air back into his lungs. He scooted backward so he could sit against the rock and regain his senses. Hearing the *swish, swish* sound out in the clearing, he got up to investigate.

The strangest, deepest growl he'd ever heard stopped him before he took a step. Wayland's first thought was *bear*, but the black bears he and his brothers hunted made huffing or grunting sounds. This growl was different: long and rattling, almost like a cat purring. He caught movement in the bushes and strained his eyes to see. *Stripes?* It was a cat, all right, but bigger than any mountain panther ever seen in these parts. *A tiger? In Kentucky?*

The big cat slunk out of the bush and sat upright on its haunches, not six feet away from Wayland, who was backed up against the rock. The tiger continued its threatening purr. When Wayland tried taking a sideways step to move along the face of the boulder, the tiger snarled nastily and clawed the air with its massive front paws, jabbing like a prize fighter. Wayland moved his right hand slowly toward his waistband, where his pistol was holstered. From overhead, maybe atop the boulder, he heard a man's soft but firm voice.

"Danté! *Épaules!*"

The tiger sprang forward and reared up. He laid his front paws on each of Wayland's shoulders and stared him straight in the face. Wayland felt hot breath and, as frightened as he was, became transfixed by the cat's yellow-green eyes. A moment later, Wayland felt a sudden warmth in the seat of his pants.

MURPH AIKENS RODE like a mad man but could not quite close the gap between himself and the girl on the big gray. Though the sky had darkened, it was easy enough to keep her in sight. She still held the torch high, leaving a trail of sparks behind her. Aikens caught glimpses of the falcon flying along, just over her head. The girl rode as if she were part of the horse, finding a way through the thick underbrush where there seemed to be none. He thought they must be close to the McCullum place by now.

Sure enough, he saw her break out of the trees only thirty yards ahead of him. When he got there, he realized they had made a wide circle and were coming up on the back side of McCullum's farm. The barn loomed ahead, and the girl disappeared through the open rear doors, torch blazing.

Aikens pulled his horse up hard, skidding to a stop. For the first time since he'd laid eyes on the girl, he felt a wave of uneasiness. *This is all too strange to be happening.*

He dismounted and let the reins drop to the ground. There were a few flickers from the torch in the doorway, then the light went out. After half a minute with no sound from inside, Aikens started walking. He stepped through the opening. The door at the other end of the barn was also open, letting in a large shaft of moonlight. There was no sign of the girl or the gray horse. He crept along, staying near a row of wood-slatted stalls to keep out of the moonlight.

From between the planks of the last stall, something long and claw-like shot out and grabbed Aikens's arm, then jerked him toward the stall. He slammed into the boards, shoulder first. A second claw reached for his other arm and spun him around so that his back was against the slats. Aikens felt the two hands move down and grasp him around the ribcage. *But too big to be hands ...*

Try as he might, Aikens could not pry the huge fingers loose. The monster grip on his ribs began to tighten, squeezing out his breath. He heard a chilling raspy whisper from the stall, and made out the word, *coward.* Aikens tried to yell but only a wheezy sound came out. There was a sharp *crack, crack,* and blinding pain as a couple of ribs fractured. Then, the hands shoved him away from the stall, sending him sprawling onto the earthen floor. Aikens gasped for breath and the busted ribs made themselves known. He sucked in just enough air to scream.

HANK DIDN'T KNOW IT, but he and Aikens were the only Avengers left in the raid. He was grateful to have been elected one of the torch bearers. He'd lost track of Lon right after they'd seen the white-faced, fire-throwing *haints* and started riding hell-bent into the forest. When he finally slowed down, he could hear the terrified cries of the other men somewhere out in the trees and didn't want to think about what had become of them. He was tempted to turn for home but didn't fancy running into the unholy creatures behind him.

Hank kept riding in a straight line and, by no fault of his own, stumbled across the lane leading to the McCullum farm. On the chance that the rest of the Avengers were there waiting for him, he pressed on. His torch began to sputter. *Not much time.*

He soon emerged into a clearing of about two acres. The moon was low and to his back, lighting the McCullum cabin off to the right and the barn and outbuildings a few hundred feet to the left. A lantern glowed a faint yellow through the cabin window. The farm was quiet, nary a raider in sight. Hank reined up. Just then, he heard an agonized scream coming from the barn, where the doors stood open. *Murph?*

Hank dug heels into his horse's sides and aimed for the barn doors. Halfway there, he saw something scurry across the clearing toward him. As it entered the circle of torch light, Hank made out the features of what looked to be a child. *In a uniform?* The figure resembled a toy soldier, running at an angle toward him with a small raised sword. In seconds, they met. The toy soldier twirled the sword overhead, then swung it under Hank's boot, severing the girth strap of his saddle as he rode by. Hank hit the ground in an instant, tumbling hat over heels.

When he was able to sit, Hank looked all around for his attacker. The torch lay a few yards away. He grabbed it and held it out from him, turning in circles. The toy soldier had vanished. Hearing a groan from the barn, Hank yelled, "Murph! I'm coming! It's me, Hank."

He was only a step away from the open door when something long and snaky reached out of the barn and curled quickly around his wrist. It began to lift him up by the arm, which still gripped the torch, until his feet left the ground. The skin of the snaky thing holding him felt leathery, hot, and bristly. It began to shake him until, finally, the sputtering torch flew from his hand. Then, the rest of the creature stepped out into the moonlight, the massive body barely fitting through the barn door opening. Hank could hardly take in the sight. Above its long, twisting nose, the face was flat and wide—bigger than any bull's—with dark wrinkly hide. Even in the near-darkness, Hank was startled by the beast's glittering eyes, like the copper of new pennies. His assessment of the creature was cut short when it let go of his wrist, dumping him into a water trough.

MURPH DREW SHALLOW BREATHS, keeping his arms close at his sides to avoid the stabs of pain. He saw something large and hulking move through the door at the other end of the barn, temporarily blocking the moonlight. A long appendage twisted over its unbelievably massive head. Murph was in too much agony to be afraid. His brain swirled from all he had seen. *What are all these creatures? The strange girl on the horse, and the fire-spewing demons. This beast with a long arm curling out of its head?*

The door to the stall across from him began to creak open. Murph was in no shape to confront the attacker who'd nearly crushed him like an acorn. *No ghost this time. Had to be Stanley. Big weak-minded lout.*

Sure enough, the shadowy figure of Stanley McCullum emerged from the darkness of the stall. He stood, looming over Murph like an oak tree. One side of him was faintly outlined in the moonlight. The fear crept back into Murph's chest. *He's even bigger than I remembered. Reckon I'm a dead man.*

"I could kill you ..."

The voice was low and hollow, like it came from the bottom of a well. *The giant had read his thoughts then.* Murph squeezed his eyes shut and waited for what would come next.

"But you ain't worth the trouble," Stanley finished. "Besides, I wouldn't want folks saying you died for your cause. I've seen some heroes, Murph Aikens, and you ain't one of them."

Murph opened his eyes. He sucked in a little air, enough to speak.

"We just meant ... to give you folks a scare. Why're you here? Thought you was ... still ..."

"Still *fighting*? Still on a battlefield somewhere dodging lead while you and your cowardly cousins ride around bullying poor country folk? You were going to burn the place. I don't call that a scare."

Murph watched Stanley's hands, clenching and unclenching.

"We're done ... with it. Mark my words." Murph's voice came in short, broken rasps. "Breaking up ... the bunch ... after tonight. Just let ... me ride out. You done broke ... half my ribs."

With a sudden great roar, Stanley shoved the heels of his hands at the stall door that Murph was propped against. The injured man threw his arms up to cover his head as a heavy wood plank over him splintered.

"Then ride out, before I break the rest of them!" Stanley boomed. He pointed to the front door. "Go gather up your last Avenger and get off our farm."

Murph struggled to stand, using the damaged stall behind him for support. "I'm going! Place is ... haunted anyways. Devil spirits all over."

"Devil?" An amused smile spread over Stanley's face. "How do you know you're not looking at him?"

It occurred to Murph that it might be true.

THE SQUARE PATCH of moonlight on the barn floor was smaller

now as the moon made its ascent. With Stanley still watching, Murph limped toward the opening. He was sure he'd heard Hank calling out earlier, but there was only silence now. That didn't give him any comfort. He peeked around the edge of the doorway. The wide clearing was empty, and the cabin windows were dark. He took a cautious step outside.

"Murph?" someone whispered. "Is that you?"

Murph looked around but saw no one. Then, he heard soft splashes to his left. Hank emerged from a water trough hat first—then head, shoulders, and torso–until he stood dripping, submerged to his mid-thighs.

"Hank! What the hell are you doing?" Murph could see Hank's eyes, wide and terrified.

"I'm hidin' my clodhopper ass, that's what I'm doing," he whispered. "Or at least playing dead. Did you see that— that thing that come out here? It got me, Murph! Picked me up with its durn nose!"

"I saw it. Had my ... own troubles. Stanley the giant. Broke some ribs, I reckon." Murph kept his voice low and tried to sound nonchalant. "I say ... we slip out of here. Try to find the others. My horse is in back. Where's yours?"

Hank pulled off his hat and wrung the water out. "Maybe Bowling Green by now. Right before that big thing grabbed a hold of me, some little wind-up soldier with a sword had run up and ..." He stopped his telling of the event, as if he knew how preposterous it must sound.

"Well, anyways—truth is, Murph, there's been some mighty spooky things going on around here. I'm ready to high-tail it, horse or not." He grabbed the edge of the trough and stepped out, water streaming down each leg. He leaned against the barn and tugged his soggy boots off to empty them.

"Amen, Hank," said Murph. "Let's try to get ... back to my horse. Might need a hand ... getting on him."

They stayed close to the outside wall of the barn and worked their way around back. Murph wasn't going to chance meeting Stanley again. Hank picked up the reins of Murph's horse and stood alongside him. He crouched and patted one knee. "See if you can step up here on my leg. Then I'll give you a push. Careful, my britches is wet."

After a couple of attempts and some swearing through gritted teeth, Murph got his hands on the saddle horn and pulled himself up. "Gawdamighty, that hurts!"

Hank handed Murph the reins and, being a small man, stuck his boot in the stirrup and hopped nimbly into place behind the cantle. Murph reined the gelding around to face the woods, but the animal began tossing its head and wouldn't take a step.

FROM OUT OF the shadows of the forest, the big gray horse appeared, neck arched and front hooves stepping high. It headed directly toward Murph and Hank. To their shock, the horse suddenly became two horses walking abreast. Then, the two became three, and Murph realized they had been walking in single file and were breaking to the left and right of the leader. At last, *four* identical gray steeds pranced side by side, their steps synchronized like the workings of a clock. The two in the middle bore riders—the girl with the long hair and another who could be her twin.

Murph and Hank sat motionless astride the gelding. The grays kept approaching and when they were only a few yards away, they split into pairs and were about to pass alongside them. Murph could see the amber eyes and parted lips of the lovely girl as she rode closer. He turned his eyes to her double, knowing the riders would soon pass on either side of him. At this distance, the second girl was strikingly similar to the first, although her eyes were not as doe-like.

This girl tossed a long lock of hair back over her shoulder, smiled fetchingly and reached for Murph just as their horses met. She slowed and wrapped her long delicate arms around him, pulling him close. Then, before he could react, the girl kissed him full on the mouth—her lips hungrily nudging his for response. Murph felt himself lean into her, the broken ribs—and Hank—forgotten. Never had he dreamed of feeling a woman offer herself to him this way.

With what seemed like reluctance, the girl finished the kiss and looked into Murph's eyes. Her skin was luminous in the moonlight. She raised one hand to the side of her head. With a sudden jerk she snatched at her hair, pulling the locks onto her lap —and in the next moment Murph was looking at the close-cropped head of—*a man?* Realization broke over Murph's face like daylight. Now he could see the strong chin, the lithe, muscled shoulders. From somewhere nearby he heard a woman's soft musical laughter.

"Stefan!" she called, "You've had your fun. Leave him alone."

The beautiful Stefan threw his head back and laughed. Then, in a swirl of dappled gray and dust, the horses stormed away in all directions, eventually disappearing into the dark woods.

MURPH HAD NEVER KNOWN it was possible to retch with a set of cracked ribs. He hung to one side of the saddle, giving it his best try. The sounds passing from his lips were both strangled coughs and guttural moans. Hank held to Murph's waistband, trying to steady him without inflicting further pain.

"We got to get out of here, Murph. They's haints all over this place. Some little, some giant. And a woman that turns into a man!"

With one last dry heave and long groan, Murph sat up as best he could. He held to the saddle horn and tried to catch his breath. "Hank," he said finally, "get reins ..."

Hank was not inclined to get off the horse and risk meeting up with another demon, but he knew it was the only way to escape the haunted place. His boots squished when he hit the ground. In seconds, he had handed the reins up to Murph and was again seated behind the saddle.

"You ain't going in the woods are you, Murph? Where them horses went?"

Murph slowly wagged his head and turned the gelding. They rode along the side of the barn and entered the clearing in front of the cabin. "Keep quiet," he warned Hank. They crossed the open space at a walk and found the lane leading away from the McCullum farm. The woods around them were pitch black. Only the tree frogs noted their passing.

GLASGOW, Kentucky
October 19, 1861

OUR DEAR STANLEY,

Your father and I were so pleased to receive your letter and to hear that you and your party arrived safely in New Orleans. We find the old farm quiet and lonesome without your presence. At evening time, we reflect on the cheerful times we spent while your traveling companions were here and even miss the day to day antics of the animals, which we knew were all in good fun. I notice that there are a few of Mary Ann's big footprints left in the barn. Your pa has been careful to see that they are not raked away or walked over. I suspect he plans to show them to some visitor one of these days— that is, if anyone dares to drop by. After the scare you all gave to Murph Aikens and his boys, we have little worry that they will set foot on the place again. I do not think any of them ever caught on that they were ambushed by a circus troupe! They must have spread stories around town since we have noticed the folks there show a change in demeanor of late. Why, I bought sewing notions at Deke Reynolds's store last week and he stared at me the entire time as if I were a leper! We have not attended any church meetings since your departure. I can only imagine what those old crones have been prattling about. (Do not worry, my son. Your pa and I are not troubled by their cold shoulders and idle talk.)

We are as ready for the approach of winter as we can be. The root cellar is half full of turnips and potatoes. Tell poor Lord Minikin that, unfortunately, there is no room for a bed there until spring. It appears that our beloved state will join the cause of the Confederacy before long. General Polk took Columbus last month. It was clever of him to stretch a mile-long chain across the river to block the Union gunboats!

Give our regards to Count Wilhelm and the rest of the group—the "astonishing host of curiosities," I believe he calls them. Of course, all are welcome to visit, should their paths bring them near to our little farm. Take care, my son, and write us when it is convenient. We think of you every day and pray you are kept from harm.

Your loving mother,

Elizabeth McCullum

P.S. We were thrilled to hear of Katerina's engagement to Count Wilhelm. They will make a handsome pair. Tell her I am happy to share my biscuit recipe (and others) with her. She is so kind to ask. E.M.

SHEEP'S CLOTHING

RUNT HORNBECK HAD NO TROUBLE SNEAKING UP ON THE SLEEPING man, in spite of having blistered feet and two days of hunger gnawing at his gut. The sky had just turned dark and the wood on the campfire burned high, popping and sparking. Runt had been honed in on that fire for the last hour—first, walking toward the smoke before sunset, then the flickers of yellow through the sage.

The man slept noisily, a long frock coat draped over his torso, and his face was covered with a flat-brimmed hat. Between him and the fire lay a 12-gauge shotgun. A nondescript bay was tied off to a nearby mesquite bush. Runt went to the horse first, running his hand along the mare's neck to quiet her nerves. He needn't have worried about waking the man, who produced a pair of staccato snores and rolled onto his side.

Runt closed his fingers around the stock of the shotgun and lifted it slowly out of the dirt. *Loaded! This'll be easy.* Once he had it trained on the sleeper, he reached down with one hand and snatched the man's coat.

"What? Say, who's ...?" The man pushed the hat off his face and sat up. His eyes widened when he realized his situation.

"Thanks for the coat. I'll be needing the hat too. Just throw it over here." Runt looked the man over for a side arm but saw none. "Stand up and turn around. You ain't got a blade on you, have you?"

"No, sir. Nothing." The man clambered to his feet and turned in a full circle, keeping his hands in the air.

"Good. Now saddle the horse. Don't forget the saddlebags, and don't forget I'm watchin' you."

The fellow was no gunman, and no cowpuncher either. Runt watched him heave the saddle onto the bay and cinch up, hands shaking a little. He positioned the saddlebags with great care.

"They're mighty stuffed. Whatcha got in there? Rob a bank or something?" Runt smirked at his own inside joke. He'd just broken out of a crumbling jail after doing that very thing.

"Only ... books. Some I sell, but not all, of course."

"Of course," said Runt, but didn't really know what he had meant. "That's all I need from you. Well, maybe the boots. Mine have breathed their last." Runt motioned the man away from the horse and leaned against it to shuck his broken-down boots. The man grimly tossed his own pair at Runt's feet.

"Not a bad fit. Don't run into many gents my size." Runt straightened to his full six feet two. He had, in fact, been the runt of the litter. Both his brothers back in Kentucky were half a head taller. His ma had said he was also the prettiest of the boys, a feature he did not appreciate the value of until much later.

"All right, my friend. Much obliged for the outfit." Runt mounted the bay and swung the shotgun around toward the man, who stood buckle-kneed by the fire. Suddenly, he took a deep breath and stood tall. "You needn't shoot me," he said. His eyes, suddenly calm and unafraid, met Runt's. "I'm no threat to you. Why, I'm only a—"

A blast from the 12-gauge ended his speech.

~

FROM THE LOOKS of the town, Runt guessed it had been there a handful of years, but probably wouldn't last much longer than that. There was light, unhurried activity at the mining operation he passed. The townsfolk appeared to be making a go of it, however, and the main street was well built-out. Frame houses lined the side streets, some with pickets in front. A few spindly rose vines clung to the corner posts.

Runt pulled up the bay. The Silver Tooth Saloon loomed tall and inviting. Too bad he had no coin—he'd done a quick inspection of the saddlebags and, sure enough, found only books and a few essentials. Maybe he would sell the books to some pretty school teacher. *Or, better yet, work out a trade ...*

A woman leading two little girls across the street first froze, then broke into a smile when she saw Runt. She quickened her steps and disappeared into a low building with a discreet sign over the door, then emerged again, followed by a man in a worn, but once-nice suit. The woman began whispering to other passersby, pointing in Runt's direction. A wave of friendliness spread across each face. *Must not get many visitors around here.* The smiling folk formed a loose crowd behind him.

The suited man approached Runt. "Well, hello. I'm Richard Keeling, the local school teacher. Welcome to Tempest! Misses Jones here said she knew it had to be you. The fact is, no one passes through here anymore, now that the silver mine is playing out. And Tempest isn't on the way to anywhere, I'm afraid. It's been two months since we received the letter that you were coming this way and, frankly, we'd begun to worry some hazard had befallen you."

Runt stared blankly at the small admiring mob. *So much for the pretty school teacher scheme.* "Sure, I'm ... I'm, uh, thrilled to be here. Yeah, there's a host of, uh, hazards out here likely to befall a man." He squirmed in the saddle and wiggled his toes inside his boots, which were a tad tight. Voices drifted from the Silver Tooth Saloon, only a few yards away. Runt touched his hat brim. "Say, I don't suppose one of you fine people could buy me a—"

"Anything you wish, brother!" Keeling extended his hands in welcome. "Our homes and our hearts are open to you. We've been so long without a preacher, we're prepared to supply any of your needs."

Preacher! Holy Moses.

A slim girl in her teens pushed to the front of the group, dragging a blushing young man by the sleeve. "We've been waiting for you to get here so we can be married. Right, William?" William grinned and looked down at his feet. "And we saved ten dollars to pay you. Show him, William." William dug inside his vest and pulled out a thin fold of bills. After thumbing through them, he held up a creased ten-dollar note.

"You never know," the girl continued, "there might be others who decide to get themselves married up while you're here in town." She glanced at a couple of young ladies off to her side. One of them covered her mouth in embarrassment. The girl's friends giggled like they were part of the conspiracy.

Runt had never been much at arithmetic. But two weddings at ten dollars a shot! And maybe even a hatpassing or two. Isn't that what preachers did? Sure, he needed a drink. Maybe he could do without liquor for the time being, or get sneaky about it. Play along with this preacher-in-town business.

To Keeling he said, "Well, I could sure use a good scrubbing and some place to stretch out. I rode all night after I – well, to get here, I mean."

"Ah! You'll stay in our quarters, my son's and mine," said Keeling. It's in back of our business. He pointed to the building he'd come out of earlier. Runt leaned forward and squinted to read the sign over the door. TEMPEST UNDERTAKER.

"Thought you said you were the school teacher."

Keeling splayed his hands in explanation. "Yes, I am the school teacher, but I am also the local undertaker. The need for those services doesn't arise frequently, but when they do ..."

"And you live in the funeral parlor. With your son."

"Yes, you'll find we have a pleasant apartment at the rear. There's a separate door so you wouldn't have to walk by the coffins, or bodies should there be any. I suppose you're accustomed to seeing the occasional dead body in your line of work, brother."

"Ah, yes, I have seen a few of those in my, uh, line of work. Reckon it's just part of it. Part of life, I mean. Right, Mr. Keeling? We live, we die." Runt wondered whether he should remove his hat for effect.

A gaggle of half-drunk cowhands pushed through the saloon doors, mumbling something about getting back to the ranch before dark. Runt felt the whiskey craving lick at his veins.

"As you can see, there are plenty of depraved souls for the saving," said Keeling. "I suppose every town has its share of drunkards. Those are Joe Shamblen's hands. I'll take your bags and show you to your room. After you've washed up, we'll walk to Sally's for supper. Best beef steak in town."

Runt followed him to the funeral parlor's rear entrance. He met the kid, nodded as Keeling showed him around the place, and finally, after pulling off his boots and flexing his smarting feet, lay back on the narrow bed, heels hanging just over the end. He stared at the ceiling, pondering his predicament. *A preacher! Reckon those were the last words that fella didn't get to say. Should've asked for a few pointers before I snuffed him. Well, I only need to know enough to collect my pay and move on.*

Runt decided to unload the saddlebags. In one, there were a

few hymnals and prayer books, several Bibles, all new except one. He opened its cover and saw a bold elegant signature on the first blank page. *Gabriel Snow. Charlottesville, Virginia.* When he turned the Bible over and shook it, pieces of paper – sermon notes, he guessed – fluttered out.

The second bag held a neatly rolled change of clothes. Runt washed up at the dry sink and put them on. He peered into the small hanging mirror, studying the face ever in need of a shave, the coal-colored hair and brows, the pale blue eyes. A killer's eyes. *You sure as hell don't look like any preacher I ever saw.*

He raked the hair away from his face, walked out to join the Keelings, and sighed. *Oh, to be among the depraved souls tonight.*

THE BOY WAS NINE, he said, and named Ezra. His eyes were the same mossy green as the Kentucky rivers in Runt's memory. There was something unsettling about him, sitting there across the table, like he was reading Runt's thoughts.

"Forgive my son for staring," said Keeling. "Ezra has never seen a minister before. He says he'd like to become one someday. It's very strange—I don't know where he got the notion." Runt finished the steak, right down to the fat rind. "Well, how about that."

Keeling continued. "Er, it must be a hard life, being a circuit rider such as yourself. We wrote the conference some time ago, asking to be added to the nearest circuit. And you know only too well how far away that is."

Runt nodded, stuffing a biscuit in his mouth.

Keeling seemed agitated at the lack of response. "The bishop told us he'd be sending one of their newer ministers. How long have you been preaching, Brother Snow?"

"Ohhh ...." Runt stared at his plate, afraid to meet Keeling's eyes, or Ezra's. Especially Ezra's. "Not long at all. Still learning the, uh, ropes."

After a silence, Keeling waved at Sally and mouthed "pie," pointing to everyone at the table. "The young couple you met, Saralee and William, are anxious to have their wedding. Perhaps they can plan it for some time before Sunday, when you deliver your sermon. We meet in the school house for worship."

Sally appeared quickly, sliding three saucers of apple pie in front of them. Runt offered a strained smile. The reality was closing in. "I reckon I'll do my best," he said, hoping he could find some direction in Snow's books regarding wedding ceremonies. And sermons.

"What will you preach about?" Ezra hadn't yet touched his pie. He'd plastered his hair into wet submission, but a cowlick was beginning to spring up on top.

"Well, I haven't given it much thought." Runt licked the cinnamon sweetness from his bottom lip. "I, uh, well, I'll have to wait and see—"

"How the Spirit leads you?" interrupted Ezra. "You're waiting for divine inspiration?"

"Now, Ezra," said Keeling. "It's impolite to ask such questions. Leave the sermon topic to Brother Snow."

Runt wiped his chin with his napkin. "No, no. I don't mind one bit. What would, uh, you suggest the sermon be about, young man? You get any inspirations from the, well, the divine Spirit?"

"Well, he is only a young boy," Keeling answered.

Ezra frowned. "David was only a boy when he got anointed. That was before he even killed the giant."

"Killed a giant!" Runt said.

"Yes, sir. You know ... Goliath."

"Goliath? Oh, yes siree. Goliath. I know all about him. That David, he killed him. Killed him plum dead."

Keeling smiled. "It's his favorite Bible story."

"Well, maybe you're the one who ought to be preaching Sunday, Ezra. You could preach about that story right there."

"Oh, no. I'm not ready yet. I don't believe my calling has happened. But it sure has been on my mind. It took David a while to get ready too."

"Say, do you even know where that Bible story is? The one about him killing that giant?" Runt took another bite, trying to appear disinterested.

Ezra sat up a little straighter. "Why, yes sir, I do. It's First Samuel, chapter seventeen," he said with great pride.

"Well, ain't you something! First Samuel, chapter seventeen. You are one smart boy." Runt finished the pie, feeling plenty proud of his own smarts. *Got to remember that. First Samuel, chapter seventeen. Huh, wonder how many of those Samuels there are?*

RUNT HAD BEEN to very few weddings. Maybe just one. Most of his cronies didn't fraternize with women of the marrying sort. But here he was, in the sight of God and several dozen witnesses, about to unlawfully join together a dewy-eyed bride and her bashful groom. Runt hadn't lost any sleep over his lack of ordination as a minister. After all, the man who proclaimed another man a preacher was but a human himself and was only a minister because somebody else said he was.

Thank goodness the real Gabriel Snow had marked crucial pages in his Book of Common Prayer and Runt found the wedding liturgy with no trouble. *All I got to do is read, and ain't it just a lucky thing that I got all the way through the sixth grade?*

The ceremony was held at the home of the bride's family. The parlor was stuffy and dark, but someone had strung some wild-flowers and ribbon on the mantel, lending a little floral relief.

Runt finished up with the back-and-forth *do-you-takes* and *have-and-holds*. That took some concentration, making sure both parties got to say their piece. Then it was on to the pronouncing them man and wife. Poor William didn't spend much time on the *kiss-the-bride* part. He gave her no more than a small peck, then pulled out a big white handkerchief and began mopping his forehead.

Runt collected his ten dollars and made a quiet exit through the back door. He didn't care to partake of the sweets and fruit punch. The pull of the Silver Tooth Saloon was especially strong after the stress of the ceremony. He thought of slipping in just for a quick one, but Ezra caught up with him outside, all big-greeneyed and asking what he thought about the Trinity.

"Ezra, I got no time to get into a deep discussion about that right now. All I got to say is that I've crossed the Trinity at its highest many a time, with no small amount of difficulty, and I've come to believe it's got a mind of its own. My advice to you ism don't go crossing the Trinity if it can be helped."

Ezra stopped walking. Runt glanced back to see the boy scratching his head, pondering the theology of what he'd just been told.

Two sisters got married side by side on Saturday afternoon, one to a cowhand and the other to a man forty years her senior. Runt suspected at least one of the unions was a marriage of coercion, maybe even both of them. The father of the brides seemed none too pleased and only paid the preacher seven dollars for the double wedding. Still, it wasn't bad money for thirty minutes of reading. The boots were beginning to stretch, so Runt had an easier time standing in one place this go-round.

He had to admit he was nervous about the Sunday sermon, and decided to stick with reading from the scripture, maybe making a few general comments that wouldn't expose his lack of knowledge.

"Old Mister Hinchey is our song leader," explained Keeling, as he and Ezra walked alongside Runt on the way to the school house. "Of course, he may or may not attend, as he was married yesterday."

"That old fella that married one of the sisters?"

"Yes, the same. He has a nice voice. Or did, when he was younger."

"Well, how about that." Runt and the Keelings reached the school just as a buckboard bounced into the yard. The couple on the seat looked stricken, as if they'd just seen some horrible sight. The man yanked on the brake pole and jumped off the wagon in a mighty leap.

"Keeling! Maggie and I were driving in for the service." He turned to Runt. "I'm Terrance Holt. Our place is a good ten miles out, so we got an early start. Anyway, we came upon a corpse. In pretty bad shape."

Holt shook his head. "Looked like he'd been robbed and shot. No horse, no coat or boots. Poor Maggie, she nearly fainted."

"A corpse!" said Keeling. "How terrible! An Indian attack, you suppose?"

"Don't think so. Only a few tracks but not from moccasins. The poor fellow took a shotgun blast up close. Not much ..." He looked back at Maggie and lowered his voice. "Not much left of his face that would identify him. He's there in the buckboard, covered up with Maggie's shawl. Well, mostly covered. He's a tall one."

A hard knot formed in Runt's belly. *Thought I'd be long gone before anybody ran across that dead preacher. Just play it nice and easy ...*

Keeling scratched his beard. "Well, there's nothing that can be done for him now. I suppose we will carry on with the church service and I will take charge of him afterwards. Perhaps you should pull your wagon around back so as not to upset everyone. There's no need to spoil the worship service with grim news." Ezra did not speak, listening to the talk of corpses as if it were nothing new.

The townsfolk arrived in small groups. The school house buzzed with friendly greetings as they all found seats. Runt sat in a straight back chair backed up to the chalk board. Snow's Bible lay on his lap. Snow himself lay outside.

Keeling opened with a few announcements about illnesses and other congregational news, then said a brief prayer. Mister Hinchey was in attendance, but without his bride, who "wasn't feeling well." He rubbed his eyes and opened a hymnal. The songs, all with numerous verses, were unknown to Runt. Hinchey's voice sounded tired and dry around the edges. When the hymns were over, he shuffled to the back row of chairs and promptly fell asleep.

Keeling proclaimed a welcome on behalf of the town of Tempest to the circuit minister, Brother Gabriel Snow. He nodded and smiled at Runt, then joined Ezra on the front row.

Don't look at the boy. Say some pretty words, pass the hat, and ride out first thing tomorrow. As Runt stood, the squeak of the rush chair seat echoed in the silent room. He stepped to the simple podium and opened the Bible.

"Much obliged for the warm welcome. We'll just get right to it.

I'm readin' from First Samuel, chapter seventeen." He waited until the page-flipping sounds died down, then began reading the chapter—fifty-eight verses long—beginning with the gathering of the Philistine and Israelite armies.

"... and there went out a champion out of the camp of the Philistines, named Goliath, of Gath, whose height was six cubits and a span."

At this point, Ezra piped up. "That's nine and a half feet tall!" Keeling shushed the boy, then patted him on the shoulder.

"Well, thank you, young man. Yep, that Goliath was one big galoot. Now, where was I?" Runt finished the chapter, reading of David felling the giant with five smooth stones and a sling and ending with the boy hero standing before King Saul, holding up the severed head of the champion Goliath.

"Now that's a fine story, folks. Just goes to show you can't judge a man by his size. That Goliath was a mean one. Why, I've known a few like him myself. And brought down by a boy! But not just any boy, I reckon."

He made the mistake of looking at Ezra. The green eyes were fixed on him, reading him. Runt felt like the shadows of a canyon feel, when the sun breaks over the rim and lights every cranny. No place to hide. *What does that boy know?*

"Well, that's about all I got to say. Can't improve on what's already been writ. You all can go home now."

An elderly man near the front whispered loudly to his wife, "He don't talk much for a preacher, does he?"

Keeling stood quickly. "Thank you, Brother Snow. If you will all please stand, I will dismiss us in prayer. Oh, and don't forget to leave your offering in the collection box near the door, where the minister will be greeting you."

Coins plunked into the collection box as Runt shook hands with the townspeople. He'd once heard there were men back east who made their money playing organs on street corners, while a trained monkey danced at their feet. Runt wondered if they felt as awkward as he did, smiling and feigning good humor, all the while watching the till and wishing to get the hell out of town.

As the people filed outside, the news of the dead man in the Holts' buckboard spread. Runt tried to slip through the crowd and head back to his room, but Keeling stopped him.

"You mentioned that you have to leave tomorrow, Brother Snow. I realize you have other obligations, but do you suppose you'd have time to conduct a brief funeral later today? We should bury this gentleman sooner than later."

"The Twenty-third Psalm is always nice at funerals," said Ezra. "It seems to bring comfort to the bereaved. Don't you agree, Brother Snow?"

The belly knot was getting bigger. Runt had the sudden notion that Keeling and Ezra – hell, maybe everyone in town knew he was an imposter and were toying with him, asking him to speak false prayers over the preacher he had murdered!

"Sure, it does. I, uh, I reckon I can do that much for him. The departed, I mean."

"Very well," said Keeling. "How about four o'clock? Late in the day, I know, but it will take me a few hours to prepare the body and dig the grave. That's well before sunset. I'll buy you another of Sally's steaks when we're done."

"Four o'clock," said Runt. "It's a deal."

I could saddle up and leave now. They'd scratch their heads for a few days and then forget about it. Or maybe it wouldn't surprise 'em at all.

The saddlebags were packed with clothing and nearly twenty-three dollars, the total take from the weddings and the church service. He left the books on the bed for Keeling and put on his coat. At the last moment, he picked up the Bible and stuck it in one of the bags, then pulled the shotgun from under the bed. *They all knew a shotgun killed the man.*

He walked out of Keeling's place and kept to the backs of the buildings, trying to get to the livery unnoticed. As he reached the horse pen behind it, a sharp *thunk* drew up him short. Ten yards away, Ezra stood holding a strap of leather in one hand. In the other he gripped a handful of rocks. He looked solemnly at Runt ... the coat and hat, the saddlebags, the shotgun pointed at the ground.

"Brother Snow. You ... leaving us?"

"Well, just gathering up my belongings. Didn't want to get caught up in the funeral and leave something behind. Whatcha doing there?"

Ezra held up the strap. "Trying to see if I could hit anything with this sling. So far, only the side of the barn, and that was on accident. It's harder than they make it sound."

"I'd imagine so. Well, I'm gonna put all this inside with the horse. I, uh, I might leave after the burying's done."

"I'll see you up at the cemetery, Brother Snow." Ezra carefully fitted another rock into the strap and slung it over his head. The stone flew straight up, then landed in the dirt not far from Runt.

"Hey, that was pretty close," said Runt. "You don't want to take out the preacher now." He winked at the boy and went into the livery barn.

RUNT WASN'T sure what made him show up at the cemetery. What good sense he had told him to ride fast and ride far. *Is it that boy?*

103

Why do I care what he thinks? There was just something pure and innocent about Ezra, like he wasn't from the regular world. Runt hadn't run across anyone like him before.

The Holts had stayed in town for the funeral, feeling some obligation since they had discovered the body. In fact, most everyone who'd been at church was there. There weren't many happenings in Tempest— two weddings, one murder, and a funeral made for a red-letter week of socializing.

Runt figured this to be his last sermon, so decided to throw in a few extra pretty words he found in the Book of Common Prayer. Once the crowd gathered around the plain wood casket beside the fresh-dug grave, he cleared his throat and began to read.

"O God, who by the glorious resurrection of your Son Jesus Christ destroyed death, and brought life and immortality to light: Grant that your servant ... whose name we, uh, whose name we don't know ... being raised with him, may know the strength of his presence, and rejoice in his eternal glory; who with you and the Holy Spirit lives and reigns, one God, for ever and ever. Amen." He turned a few pages and continued.

"The LORD is my shepherd; I shall not want. He maketh me to lie down in green pastures: he leadeth me beside the still waters." Ezra had been right. Runt found his nerves settling as he quoted the words of the psalm.

"Yea, thought I walk through the valley of the shadow of death, I will fear no evil: for thou art with me; thy rod and thy staff they comfort me."

Runt paused, remembering something. *Gabriel Snow wasn't scared, there at the last. I had a shotgun pointed at him. He said I needn't shoot him, he was no threat to me. But he said it calm, like he was just stating facts. 'Though I walk through the valley of the shadow of death, I will fear no evil.' Evil. He didn't fear it. He didn't fear me.*

He kept reading. "Thou preparest a table before me in the presence of mine enemies: thou anointest my head with oil; my cup runneth over. Surely goodness and mercy shall follow me all the days of my life: and I will dwell in the house of the LORD forever."

So somewhere, there might be a house of the Lord, and Gabriel Snow could be seated at a table at this very minute looking down on Runt Hornbeck's sorry ass pretending to be him.

Runt looked at the casket. *Makes you wonder who's the lucky one.* He glanced around at the townsfolk of Tempest, sorrowful for a man they didn't even know. *Maybe he ought to fess up. Who would he be when he rode out of town? Back to his old name and ways?* Runt Hornbeck was a wanted man. But to carry on this preacher business! There was a little money in it. There was also a *lot* of walking the line.

Ezra startled everyone by speaking up, his voice sweet and clear. "Brother Snow, would you mind if I spoke a few words? And may I borrow your Bible?"

Runt felt like Goliath must have, seeing the stone just before it sank into his forehead. Thinking of Gabriel Snow, he took a deep breath and prepared for the blow. "I reckon I have no objection. Say what you got to say."

Ezra opened the Bible, taking only seconds to find what he was looking for. "I'll be reading from the book of Ephesians, chapter four," he announced.

"But ye have not so learned Christ; If so be that ye have heard him, and have been taught by him, as the truth is in Jesus: That ye put off concerning the former conversation the *old* man, which is corrupt according to the deceitful lusts; And be renewed in the spirit of your mind; And that ye put on the *new* man, which after God is created in righteousness and true holiness."

Ezra looked up for a moment, his eyes locking with Runt's, then resumed.

"Wherefore putting away lying, speak every man truth with his neighbour: for we are members one of another. Be ye angry, and sin not: let not the sun go down upon your wrath: Neither give place to the devil. Let him that stole steal no more: but rather let him labour, working with his hands the thing which is good, that he may have to give to him that needeth. Let no corrupt communication proceed out of your mouth, but that which is good to the use of edifying, that it may minister grace unto the hearers. And grieve not the holy Spirit of God, whereby ye are sealed unto the day of redemption. Let all bitterness, and wrath, and anger, and clamour, and evil speaking, be put away from you, with all malice: And be ye kind one to another, tenderhearted, forgiving one another, even as God for Christ's sake hath forgiven you. Amen."

The boy closed the Bible and handed it back to Runt. The townspeople seemed puzzled. It was Keeling who spoke. "Thank you, Ezra. Those are compelling words, and a worthy reminder to us all."

Runt wished he could crawl into the hole intended for the man in the casket – the real Gabriel Snow. Had Ezra chosen those scriptures by chance, or was the boy challenging him directly, to trade the old man for the new?

Sally, who ran the restaurant, invited everyone over for a free slice of pie—chokecherry was today's special. The crowd moved away, leaving Runt, Keeling, and Ezra standing at the graveside.

"Well, I'll finish the burial if you'd like to join the others," said Keeling. "Or perhaps you'll be leaving now. Ezra said you might."

Runt ran his hand over the Bible cover, then laid it on a nearby headstone. "Reckon I'll help you out, if you've got an extra shovel."

"IT WILL SOON BE DARK," said Keeling. "You are welcome to stay another night."

Runt led the saddled horse out of the barn. "Many thanks, but I'd just as soon get going. Don't mind making camp." He shook Keeling's hand. "Obliged for the hospitality. Not sure whether we'll meet again. The, uh, head office might be sending you another preacher next time around."

"Oh, I'm sorry to hear that. Well, Godspeed to you, Brother Snow."

Ezra stood quietly at his father's side. Runt bent over to shake his hand. "You're quite a boy, Ezra Keeling. I got a notion you'll do mighty big things." The boy nodded, as if accepting an order.

He rode south. There were plenty of places to choose from in that direction. All of Texas. Mexico. Maybe turn west to New Mexico or Arizona. He hadn't tried California yet.

He thought about the David and Goliath story again. The boy Ezra hadn't brought down big Runt Hornbeck with a stone. He'd done something else—something Runt couldn't understand just yet. There were plenty of miles ahead to ponder it.

That Goliath had the whole army fooled, just like him and the folks of Tempest. Then, a brave little boy stepped up with his sling. In Runt's mind, young David must have had mossy green eyes and a cowlick.

COMANCHE WINTER

DAMN THIS SNOW. HANK CASTLEBERRY SLUMPED IN THE SCHOOL desk and stretched out one lanky leg, then the other. *I'm too old to be going to school. Near about fifteen, I am.*

"Hank, please ... sit up straight." Schoolmaster Guilford Peach paused his discussion of past participles, waiting silently until Hank complied.

I'd druther be chopping firewood, even feeding hogs. Close to a foot of snow had blown in overnight and, after he had cleared off the steps and brought in wood, Ma told him he might as well get a day of schooling instead of sitting home all day. Hank went to school less and less, now that he was big enough to do man's work along with Papa.

In the row next to him, two blonde heads rotated in his direction, and two pairs of sky blue eyes gave him a shy side look. *Well, at least there's Alice and Ada.*

The Mitchell twins were maybe a year younger than Hank, and he was sweet on one of them, although he could never quite remember which one. It seemed to him that Alice was a touch sweeter than Ada, but they looked so much alike, down to the freckles on their noses, he had a tough time keeping them straight.

"Seth Neal, would you please give us an example of a past participle, as used in a sentence?"

A chubby boy in loose, patched pants and suspenders stood and cleared his throat. "The dog ... the dog has kilt a rabbit."

Mr. Peach nodded and grimaced. "Good, Seth. However, it's killed, not kilt. But thank you." Seth rubbed the embarrassment from his face with a pudgy hand and sat down. The schoolmaster smoothed his wavy wheat-colored hair, a frequent habit, and turned to the chalkboard. "All right, ladies and gentlemen," he said, writing a string of crisp numbers and mathematical symbols, "we're on to other things. Please solve this equation."

Since Hank hadn't been to school in months, he strained to remember what to do with the numbers and marks written on the board. Alice, or maybe Ada, twisted around to whisper to her twin. They both glanced at Mr. Peach, who still had his back to them. One of the girls giggled, but Hank couldn't tell which one.

Hank's gaze drifted to the window and the feathers of hoarfrost gathered at the corners of the panes. The potbelly stove in the center of the schoolhouse never quite warmed the edges of the room on wintry days.

Across the snow-whitened plains, Hank spied movement – a line of dark figures appearing atop a swell of the frozen landscape. He squinted. Then, he jumped to his feet, turning over the desk, and rushed to the window. With a quick rub on the glass, he peered outside and across the snow.

"Comanches!" he barked, not even noticing the adolescent break in his voice. "Three of 'em! No, four!"

A few children screamed, and Mr. Peach hurried to Hank's side. The schoolmaster's mouth hung open for a moment before he whispered, "Oh, dear God."

"Maybe they're just passin' by," said Hank, although the four riders rode on a straight and steady line for the schoolhouse. "Or wantin' food. They don't look like they're on ... on a raid."

Guilford Peach nudged Hank to the side of the window, and he moved opposite, peeking past the edge of the frame. The children, five girls and three boys, huddled behind the wood stove.

"All right." Mr. Peach raked his hair. "Hank, get everyone below, quickly. I will ... I will go outside and ... have a word with them. That is, unless they ride past."

The farmers who built the schoolhouse left space under the floors, and a few loose planks beside the teacher's desk. There wasn't room for a grown person to stand but, more than once, the class had huddled underneath in safety during fitful Texas weather.

"No, sir. I feel like I oughta stay up here," Hank said softly. "At least, till you ... get back. In case ..."

They both knew the gravity of that "in case." Mr. Peach looked at Hank, then back toward the approaching Comanches. They were now a hundred yards out.

"Seth, move the planks and help everyone hide below. Now!" The schoolmaster ducked past the window and rushed to the coat hooks by the door. He gathered his students' coats and shawls in his arms, and tossed them to the children cowered behind the old potbelly. "Here, take your coats along." He then went for his own gray woolen coat and hat.

Seth Neal worked quickly and without a word. He shoved the desk aside and, sticking his finger into a knothole, lifted two thick pine planks, exposing the dark opening to the crawl space. He gently lowered the smaller children first, then held out his hand for the Mitchell twins. Seth locked eyes with Hank, who motioned for him to go on below. The boy sighed. He eased into the opening, one leg at a time, and Hank watched Seth's head lower, his sturdy hands reaching up, grasping one board and dragging it into place. The other, he left unmoved.

Mr. Peach buttoned the collar of his coat, put on gloves and hat, and cracked open the door. A blast of cold blew in, bringing with it swirls of snowflakes. Hank saw the man take a deep breath before pulling the door open and stepping outside, heard his boots crunch on the snow, down the steps, and around the corner of the schoolhouse.

The Comanches had nearly reached the iron water pump. Hank could make out details of the foursome ... they were all young. Three wore blankets around their shoulders. One, a dark robe, maybe buffalo hide. No paint marked their faces, no weapons in hand.

Guilford Peach crossed the opening between the schoolhouse and the Indians and, when he reached the water pump, he grasped the handle and stood, feet planted apart. Hank saw that his breaths came heavy, from the rise of his shoulders and the puffs of white at his face. The schoolmaster appeared to speak first, gesturing with his free hand. The Comanches sat, listening, their horses occasionally shifting weight to one front leg, then the other. A shaggy bay dropped its muzzle to the snow and blew sharply, sending a spray of snowflakes into the air.

Hank glanced at the floor opening and saw the shadowy form of Seth Neal's face framed between sturdy knees. The boy had positioned himself so he could watch Hank. The children, the room ... all silent. A burning log shifted in the wood stove, and Hank's heart lurched.

Outside, Guilford Peach stood motionless, as if waiting for a response from the four Comanche men. He didn't have to wait long.

The Indian wearing the buffalo robe pulled up on the rope reins, and his horse tossed its head and high-stepped backward. On an unspoken command, the three others heeled their mounts and rode in a tight circle around Mr. Peach. Hank couldn't see the schoolmaster for the blur of running horses and plumes of flying snow. Buffalo Robe joined the circle, and Hank watched as the Indian bent to the side, then broke out of the formation. In the crook of his arm, he held Guilford Peach by the neck, dragging him alongside his horse, riding in erratic circles around the school yard.

The schoolmaster's hat lay near the water pump where he had been standing. Hank stepped back from the window in horror. The Comanches were shouting now ... in high, unholy cries. Buffalo Robe, still riding, held up a stone-headed war club with hair streaming from its bottom end. *Horsehair? Human?* Hank barely had time to register the thought before the Indian brought the club down and smashed Mr. Peach's temple. Blood sprayed. Mr. Peach, who had been struggling, went limp. The unholy cries escalated. One of the other Indians rode alongside Buffalo Robe and grabbed the schoolmaster's body by one leg and commenced dragging him in a loop around the water pump, leaving a ragged streak of red in the fresh snow.

Hank felt his heart pounding, and a sharp tingling around his mouth. His knees went slack. He leaned on a desk to keep from falling. *Do something ... now!*

With no idea how long the Comanches would toy with Peach's body, Hank wildly searched the schoolroom. The schoolmaster carried no weapon, had ridden no horse. The Mitchell twins' father, Lon, had brought Mr. Peach and the students to school in his wagon, because of the snowstorm.

Hank's eyes darted from object to object in the simply furnished schoolroom. *Chalkboard, eraser. Desks, Mr. Peach's the largest. A chair, books on a shelf. A coal oil lamp on the desk, unlit. The potbelly stove, a few sticks of wood. Portrait of George Washington. A framed Whitman poem.*

Hank knew he might have only seconds to act. He scanned the room once more and sucked in a breath as a thought skittered through his brain. There were maybe ten student desks. He ran across the room, gathering desks, then piling them against the door. More in front of the single window, stacked to at least slow down the Comanches if they tried entering there. He ran to the schoolmaster's desk and snatched the oil lamp.

From the whoops and yelps of the Comanches, Hank knew they were still riding circles in the school yard and hadn't closed in around the building yet. It wouldn't take them long to try breaking in once they stopped their celebrating.

Hank hurried to the potbelly stove and opened the door, searing his fingers on the hot iron latch. He shook the hand to cool the pain, then pulled a log from the bucket of firewood next to the stove. After a quick stir of the coals inside, Hank threw the log inside, followed by the coal oil lamp, which he tossed in on its side. In seconds, the glass globe burst. The coal oil immediately caught fire, filling the stove's cavity with black smoke.

Hank grabbed another log and slammed it against the stove pipe, breaking it loose from the potbelly. Thick, black smoke roiled from the opening and into the room, stinging Hank's eyes and nose. *Burn, burn! Come on, let's see some smoke!*

He crouch-walked to the crawl space opening, lifted the plank with his foot, and jumped straight down, hoping his boots didn't land on a child. Seth had made sure there was room for him and, after ducking into the cramped space, Hank reached for the planks, slid them over the opening and into place. He fumbled in his pocket for his wadded-up handkerchief and stuffed it into the knothole.

"Cover your faces with your coat sleeves!" he told the school children, although he couldn't see any of them. Silently, he praised those farmers who built the schoolhouse. Not only did they floor the building with thick, heavy planks, but they left almost no space between the boards. They had skirted the log structure with stones, affording more protection.

Even so, the stench from the burning coal oil burned at noses and throats. Hank heard a few muffled coughs. The children seemed to recognize the need for silence.

ONE OF THE other three had taken the scalp. With long and curled light hair, it would impress the women. From the edge of the school yard, Buffalo Robe sized up the log structure. A tendril of smoke rose from the pipe on the roof. *Others inside, or only the man?* He pointed to the school with the war club and let out a whoop, and when Buffalo Robe's horse sprang forward, the rest fell in behind.

THE EERIE WAR cries had stopped, but Hank still heard the Comanches' horses trampling in the school yard. For a moment, even that sound subsided. After a breathless silence, the unholiest war whoop yet pierced the air. The hair on Hank's arms stood up. He heard, then felt, the rumble of hooves as the horses neared the schoolhouse. It was harder to breathe as smoke filled the room above. The children stifled coughs and sobs. Hank reached out in the dark to comfort the small ones nearby, hoping they could all hang on long enough for the Indians to move on. *Please ... let them move on.*

BUFFALO ROBE DISMOUNTED and crept up the steps to the school-house door. Hearing no sounds inside, he gave it a push. When the door didn't budge, he put a shoulder to it and tried again. It barely moved, so he tried kicking and, this time, shoved the door open a few inches. Instantly, pitch black smoke boiled through the opening and into his face. He staggered back, confused. Another warrior walked his horse to the side of the building. The window looked dark and, when he bashed his war club into the glass, more smoke rolled out. He shouted to Buffalo Robe, who covered his face in the crook of his elbow and tried to push in through the partially opened door.

Once inside, it was impossible to see anything, and he stumbled over a piece of furniture. The black smoke took his breath and he backed up, feeling for the door frame, and finally he emerged into the cold air.

He said, as much to himself as to the other Comanches, "The man set a fire? Or … the ones inside … would burn themselves?"

"They are not worth the trouble," another said. "Leave them."

Buffalo Robe paused, his brow furrowed with indecision. The smoke was not letting up. He reached for the latch and pulled the door closed.

"I agree. Let them burn," he said. He leaped onto his horse and jerked the mustang's head to the side. As one, the four Indians rode away, pushing their mounts as fast as they could go through the knee-deep snow.

LON MITCHELL FOUND THEM. Late that afternoon, he was driving the wagon back to collect the children and Guilford Peach, and saw faint curls of black smoke coming from the window of the school-house. The snow below the window was blackened with soot, as if a fire had been burning for some time, but the building looked undamaged from the outside. As he got closer, he saw the school-master's body sprawled in the yard, with streaks and patches of blood spread across the churned-up snow. Lon felt a sickening knot form in his gut.

He jumped down from the wagon and hurried to the door, faltering in the snowdrifts. Heavy with dread, Lon pushed on the door and it opened a bit before it thudded against something hard. He knew the Comanche ways, what they did to people. It took a few hard shoves to open the door wide enough for Lon to enter, and he steeled himself for what he might find.

Everything inside was blacked over by soot but, except for the piles of desks at the window and door, the schoolroom appeared to be in perfect order. George Washington's portrait hung straight in its usual spot, though the president's features were smoked over and unrecognizable. Three books were stacked neatly in the center of the schoolmaster's desk. Lon pictured the poor man placing them there at the beginning of the school day. The acrid sting of coal oil hung on the air, and Lon pulled his neck scarf over his mouth and nose. The children were nowhere to be seen. *Taken hostage?*

"What the hell happened here?" he said softly.

HANK SHUSHED the children when he heard someone open the door. They had waited for an hour, to make sure the Comanches were gone for good. Slow footsteps sounded on the floor above their heads. One man, wearing heavy boots. Then, a soft exclamation. Not Comanche ... English!

"What the hell happened here?"

Hank had never been so glad to hear a voice. He gently raised the plank covering their hiding spot and said, "H–hello?"

LON MITCHELL LIFTED the smaller schoolchildren into the wagon and tucked blankets around their bodies. They were all jabbering at once, recounting the Comanche attack with each other and to Lon. Despite grimy faces, their smiles were wide and beaming, eyes sparkling.

"All right, where are my girls?" He turned to see Alice and Ada holding hands and shyly talking to Hank. At their father's call, they ran toward the wagon, blonde hair flying.

Hank had just told the twins he reckoned this would be his last day of school. Earned his final grade, he thought. One of the girls – he wasn't sure which one – stopped and spun around. She ran back to where Hank stood and, before he knew what happened, she planted a quick kiss on his cheek. In seconds, she had caught up to her sister.

Hank felt his entire face flush.

Gosh. I sure hope that was Alice.

THE GOLDEN MARE

"I'D GIVE HALFA THIS GOLD ... FOR A TASTE OF WATER RIGHT NOW."
Ike's voice was no more than a croak. The only thing that kept
him trudging forward through the afternoon scorch was the
pursuit of flimsy shade thrown from the horse Paxton was riding.
Soon it would be Ike's turn in the saddle. It was a lousy tradeoff...
either take a load off his boots and ride in the open sweltering sun
or dodge some of its direct heat by walking alongside in the blis-
tering sand, keeping the horse between him and the unrelenting
sun.

"There's got to be a creek up here sommers," said Paxton. "I
seen a row of cottonwoods way off when we topped that last rise.
We gone have to stop for a bit, Ike. The horse ain't gone make it."

"Hell with the horse. She's bad luck. I still don't know why in
the hell you had to go and steal a dadblamed palamina."

"Well, for one thing, she was the only horse that pore-ass
rancher had for me to steal. And look at her. She is a purty thing,
you got to admit."

Ike huffed. "And ever damn posse in Arizona Territory will
spot us a hunnerd miles off. Look at that! It's Paxton Porterfield

118

and Ike Lee DeWitt and that shiny gold horse they stole! See her gleamin' against the sky?"

"Shut yer yap, Ike," said Paxton. "What do you perpose we do? Carry these bags of double eagles to Mexico ourselves?"

Ike had no retort. Truth was, neither of them was a respectable horseman. Paxton had run his horse lame after the robbery which led to the stealing of the blonde mare. Ike's horse had succumbed to the heat a few miles back from where they were now, wherever that was.

Paxton pulled up the reins near a clump of prickly pear cactus and got off the palomino. The exhausted mare lowered her head, in no need of tethering.

"Say, Ike. I hear them Apaches drink outa this cactus when they're on the move. Just cut 'em open and there's juice inside."

"Well, I reckon that's bull. And don't say *Apaches* too loud. We got us enough troubles already."

CAL AND BELINDA GORHAM sat at each end of the table, their four comely children on benches at the sides.

"Will you return thanks, Georgie?" said Belinda.

"Yeth, Mama." Three-year-old Georgie said a brief but solemn prayer, ending with "in Jeethuth name, ayyyymen." His older sisters Betsy and Christina and brother Caleb stifled giggles. Georgie would someday outgrow his babyish speech but, for now, it provided the family with continual entertainment.

"Oh, I awmost fowgot!" said Georgie. He bent his head quickly and clasped his pudgy hands. "Pwease tell the bad men who took Bwondie fum us to bwing her back. Ayyymen again!"

Cal smiled. "Thank you, son. I'm sure the Lord is looking after Blondie, wherever she is."

. . .

THEY DUG INTO THEIR DINNER, which had been mostly hen eggs and corn lately. Today, Belinda had sliced a melon she'd been tending for weeks and the children were anxious to enjoy the juicy dessert.

Cal chewed absently, his mind on other things. He needed to go into Tucson. He was low on shotgun shells and that put a damper on hunting. They'd been out of coffee for days. Never mind the busted fence that needed wiring together if he meant to hang on to his few cattle. With Blondie gone, the Gorhams were cut off. They would have to wait for a distant neighbor to wander by to rescue them. And nobody relished riding in these far-flung parts since the stage had been run off the trail and robbed last week. The driver was shot dead. Both horses were so tangled in the harness and cactus in the ditch, they had to be put down.

Sheriff Lang had come by the next day to tell Cal he'd discovered another horse near their place, limping and thirsty and presumably belonging to the robbers. It was no coincidence that Blondie had gone missing the night before, Cal thought. He didn't want to consider the shabby treatment Blondie might be receiving about now. And he would not mention it to the young ones, who loved the mare as a pet. She had been a wedding gift from his father-in-law, and Cal hated to admit the horse was a constant reminder to him that his beautiful wife deserved better than a hard life on this decrepit little ranch.

"Cal? Cal, did you hear me?" It was Belinda. The deep contemplations scattered from Cal's mind like a covey of quail.

"I asked you to walk with Betsy and Caleb to the creek for water. I don't want them going alone."

"Yes, yes. Sorry, my dear. I'm going," said Cal. "I'm going."

"LIKE I SAID, *BULL!*"

Ike watched Paxton gingerly try to slice a saucer-sized cactus pad lengthwise with his pocket knife. The spines were, for the most part, invisible and Paxton kept yelping as they pricked his fingers. He was dauntless, however. It took him several minutes but he succeeded in halving the flat green pad. Slowly, he flipped the top slice back to reveal the moist inner flesh. He spread the halves onto a low flat rock, located conveniently in Blondie's shadow, and spread his hands in admiration of his own handiwork.

"Bull, you say?" said Paxton. "Looky there, my doubtful friend." He leaned down and took a careful lick of the prickly pear's innards.

"Well?" asked Ike.

Paxton smacked his lips and pondered a moment. "Okry. Or green pepper, maybe. By gawd, don't make no difference to me. It's close enough to water for my purposes." He leaned down again and began to slurp noisily.

"What if it's poison? Have you thought about that?" Ike was still suspicious.

Paxton looked up and grinned with bits of jellyish green clinging to his lips. "Ike, I don't reckon them Apaches has lived here this long by eatin' somethin' poison. Sides that, I'm so damn thirsty I don't care if it does kill me. Least I won't go out with a craw full of sand."

Ike watched for signs of convulsions or biliousness. When they did not present within a reasonable time, he said, "Hey, save me some, would ya?"

"Like hell!" said Paxton. "Peel yer own damn cactus."

"I ain't got no knife."

"Well, Ike. Anybody comes out in this country ort to at least carry a knife. My gawd, I cain't be takin' care of you out here!"

"Takin' care of *me*? You was the one that run them stage hosses into the ditch. We was supposed to use them to replace our tired ones. And who give you a ride when yer old nag finally laid down?"

Paxton licked the knife clean. "Oh, well, and I reckon I was the one who shot the driver between the eyes instead of knockin' him out like we talked about. Now...*now* we're wanted for robbery *and* murder!"

Ike would have countered but his tongue was like a stick of dry kindling in his mouth.

"Just give me the damn pocket knife, Paxton. No use gettin' selfish after all we been through."

"Nope. You come unperpared. You'll die unperpared. You're becomin' more and more of a hindrance to me."

The blood rose in Ike's already overheated brain. He clenched both fists, then lunged for Paxton, who was still bent over the rock.

"A hindrance, am I? You good fer nothin ..."

The swear words and family curses mingled as the two men tussled on the flat rock. Occasionally, one would roll over the slices of prickly pear and the curses would extend to all members of the cactus family as well.

Paxton and Ike, who was the bulkier of the two, struggled for control of the pocket knife. Each man's life, or death, depended on possession of the little three-inch blade ... either for the purposes of killing the other, or surviving in the harsh wasteland.

They tumbled off the rock and landed in a heap under Blondie, who had been standing quietly during the ruckus. The mare squealed and took flight, vaulting the clump of prickly pear and heading back in the direction of Tucson, with the saddle and two bags of twenty-dollar gold coins still strapped to her back.

Paxton and Ike sat up and turned their gritty, disbelieving mugs toward the plume of dust rising behind her.

DAWN SPREAD SOFTLY across the Gorham ranch. Low-slanting, golden rays bathed the fence rails and the eastern sides of the house and outbuildings. Belinda was already clearing Cal's breakfast dishes while he slipped into work boots, preparing for another day's work.

Belinda followed her husband outside to take in the sunrise. They both stopped beyond the door in total surprise, There, covered with burrs and dust and scratches, stood Blondie, contentedly munching the sparse dry grass at the edge of the stoop.

"Oh, Cal!" Belinda's voice quivered. They went to the mare, hands outstretched, touching her head and her battered legs and matted, filthy mane. She appeared to be generally sound, just very weary and in need of cleaning up.

Cal inspected the saddle and opened one saddlebag.

"What is it?" said Belinda, seeing his face turn pale.

"I believe it's the gold stolen from the stage. There must be hundreds, maybe over a thousand coins...yes, they're in the other bag too." Cal was incredulous, having never seen that amount of money.

"Oh, my heavens," said Belinda. She took a look for herself. "Ha. It's too bad we have to turn it in, isn't it, Cal?" She flashed a mischievous smile.

"Yes, too bad." He cocked his head to one side. "But ..."

"What? Whatever are you thinking?"

.   .   .

"WELL ... according to Sheriff Lang, the stagecoach line did post a reward for the safe return of the money. At least, I am quite sure he said that. Maybe not. No. He did mention something about a reward."

Belinda pounded on Cal's chest. "How much? Don't torture me like this. How much is the reward?"

Cal loved getting Belinda worked up over things. "I believe he said ... five .. hundred ... dollars."

Belinda covered her mouth with her hands and said, through the spaces between her fingers, "Oh, my heavens. Oh, my heavens." Then she threw her arms around Blondie's dust-covered neck and hugged her tightly.

"Makes you wonder," Cal said, "about the robbers. Well, horse thieves. If only Blondie could talk."

NOAH RAINS

EPHRAIM TELLER RODE IN A WIDE CIRCLE, TAKING A LAST LOOK AT the cattle before heading home. They were bunching up for the night, tired from pawing through a foot of snow all day for mouthfuls of brown, frozen grass.

It had taken four years to build the beef herd up to seventy-five head. In the fall, he'd bought six Jerseys, aiming to sell milk to a few neighbors and maybe the hotel in town, depending on the yield. Ephraim was no cattle baron but he'd made a good start in a place where many ranchers were struggling.

One heifer had calved earlier in the week and several others looked about ready. Ephraim thought the little fellow should be coming along a little better. He seemed to be nursing often but having trouble gaining weight. The mama's udder looked fine, with no sign of infection.

The horse nickered, ready to leave. Ephraim knew he was not fond of being out after dark.

"All righty, Tip. Let's go home." Tip's ears pricked at the word. Ephraim didn't have to give him a nudge from heel or rein; they were off at a trot toward feed and warm beds.

Lenora had beef stew and biscuits on the table when he trundled in, shedding his boots and coat inside the door.

"How does it look out there?" she said.

"White. Still just the one calf. He looks a little puny. Might move them into the barn tomorrow."

Lenora nodded. "Be a shame to lose the first one."

Ephraim did not answer her. *A shame to lose the first one.* Lenora would know.

And the second and third ones were hell too. He saw her pursed lips before she turned back to the wood stove.

A RAW WIND greeted him the next morning. Tip stepped calmly into the herd and, once Ephraim dropped a noose around the mama cow's neck, the horse began cutting her out to the edge. The cow tried to run for a stand of trees but Ephraim quickly dally-wrapped the rope to the saddle horn. Tip stiffened his front legs and leaned back to tighten the slack. The cow's head jerked sideways and she stopped quick. Her calf hobbled in confused circles around her, the snow up to his belly.

"Attaboy, Tip."

Beyond the mama and calf, Ephraim spied tracks in the snow leading to the woods. He tied off the lariat and hopped down, knowing Tip would stand his ground until told otherwise.

The prints were not from cattle or coyote. They had to be human but appeared to be made by someone dragging both feet ... *carrying something, maybe?* Ephraim surveyed the herd. If a cow had either calved or been butchered during the night there would have been a bloody mess. There was only trampled snow.

He walked a few yards into the trees and stopped. The tracks continued in an erratic line running roughly north. The nearest farm in that direction belonged to Harold Rains, a man Ephraim had only met a couple of times. Rains was rumored to be a fine horse trainer and spent summer months trapping free-roaming mustangs. He broke the horses to ride and sold them to the cavalry troops at Fort Reno.

But this was no time to chase after a mystery. There was no harm done that Ephraim could see and he needed to get the cow and calf back to the barn. The sharp wind pelted his face with new snowfall.

"Ephraim! Wake up. I heard the calf bawling."

He could not see Lenora but felt her warmth at his side. "What? What's wrong with the calf?" He sat up and rubbed his face.

"I don't know. There might be something in the barn."

Ephraim fumbled for his pants and boots in the dark. In a moment, he was bundled up and outside, toting a carbine. The ground and barn roof were mantled in white. Even in his haste, he felt its peacefulness.

The snow had hardened and crunched only a little as he walked to the barn. The door stood open by a couple of feet. Gripping the rifle, he slipped inside and heard a noise coming from the stall where he'd put the cow and calf. He eased toward it until he could hear a *ping ping ping* ... the sound of milk hitting the inside of a metal pail.

Ephraim rounded the corner of the stall and shouted, "Who's there?"

To his surprise, it was a skinny boy who spun around to face him, nearly upsetting the milk pail. The kid inhaled sharply. His eyes looked huge in his freckled face. Ephraim lowered the rifle and the boy's wide stare followed the barrel until it pointed straight down.

"Why are you stealing my milk?"

The boy shook his head. "Oh, no sir. Not stealing. Not...not really. Figured I was only borrowing since the cow was with a calf. I been careful to leave some for him."

Ephraim looked him over. "Well, that ain't the way it always works. It's wintertime. You...you don't know much about cattle do you, son?" The endearment stirred something in his chest.

The boy shifted nervously and ran a bony hand through shaggy blonde hair. "No sir. Reckon I don't know much about cattle."

"You belong to Harold Rains?"

"Y – yes, sir. He ... he's my pa." The boy grew more uncomfortable.

"Well ..." Ephraim was unsure of his next move. "Let's get out of this cold barn. We can talk about this in the house. What's your name?"

"It's Noah, sir. Noah Rains."

"Noah Rains? Well, that's a strange name to give somebody."

"Yes, sir. It is kindly strange. My ma got it out of the Bible. The Noah part."

"And you're how old?"

"Eleven and then some, sir."

Ephraim would have guessed eight or nine. "Well, don't forget your milk, Noah Rains."

Ephraim motioned for the boy to go ahead of him. When they passed Tip's stall, Ephraim said, "Hmph. Thought you'd be watching over the place. Never heard a squeak out of you."

Noah set down the pail and raised his thin hands to Tip's muzzle, placing one at each side of the horse's nostrils, stroking gently with his thumbs. "Oh, we're fine friends, ain't we? Tip? Is that your name? You're a good one, I can tell." The horse lowered his head and gently nudged Noah.

It was not like Tip to make friends easily. Ephraim followed the boy out into the snow and toward the house. From the looks of the billowing stovepipe, Lenora had a good fire going.

For not knowing much about cattle, looks like he speaks some horse.

~

LENORA BEGAN COOKING ALMOST AS SOON as she'd been introduced to the scrawny freckled boy. Noah ate three scrambled eggs and a thick slab of salt pork before he looked up. She had fried another three and he seemed tempted to keep eating.

Instead, he said, "Do you reckon I could take them with me? I mean, if you ... are you going to let me go?"

Ephraim sat on a stool near the stove, watching. "Aw, sure, you can go. I can always come hang you after sunup." When he saw the boy's stricken expression and Lenora's frown, he added, "Settle down, Noah Rains. That was just a sorry joke."

Lenora cleared her throat. "Why don't you just finish these off, Noah. They won't pack up well and they'll be cold by the time you get home. I'll send along some eggs and pork for your ma to cook later. The hens are laying pretty good in the barn so you'd be doing me a service."

Ephraim was always amazed at Lenora's ability to sense a person's thoughts. It made him feel even worse about teasing the boy. *She would've made a good ma.*

Noah seemed conflicted but finally agreed. "I better be getting back ... before..."

"Before your folks figure out you're gone, I reckon," said

Ephraim. Noah said nothing. Lenora helped him back into his tattered coat.

"Wish you could stay the night," she said, "but I know ..."

"Thank you, m'am. And thank you for the meal."

Ephraim waited at the door. "I'll saddle up Tip. I, for one, don't care to slog for a mile through the snow. Oh ... and don't forget your milk, Noah Rains."

MOON AND SNOW lit the way to the Rains homestead. If not for the thin ribbon of smoke rising from the chimney, Ephraim would have thought the small cabin was one of the outbuildings. It sat a ways apart from three or four horse pens of various sizes. There was a granary sided with wood slabs and low pole shed, open at one end.

Noah hopped down and started for the cabin with his cloth-bound bundle of food and the pail of milk, which had frozen. He clearly did not want Ephraim to ride any closer. After a few steps, he looked back. "Thank you, Mr. Teller ... for everything."

Ephraim could only nod and touch his hat brim. He was choked up and didn't quite know why. The boy disappeared inside the cabin. Before the door shut, Ephraim thought he glimpsed a couple of small pale figures ... their arms around Noah's legs.

THREE DAYS PASSED with no sign of milk-borrower tracks leading to the barn. The skies were clear but the temperature had dropped considerably. Ephraim had brought in the cows with the roundest bellies – just in time, it turned out. He and Lenora were up delivering calves for two nights straight. Why the act of birthing seldom occurred in daylight hours, Ephraim would never know.

The two of them talked less than usual. They were both worn down. Ranching was never easy; carrying out chores with winter's grip around them was even harder. Lenora melted snow in a dishpan on the stove. The last of the calves, for now, had made her appearance, bringing the total to seven. Cleanup was an ongoing task. Ephraim came inside from hanging washed clothes on a fence rail. The cold wind would freeze his pants into some strange shapes but they would be mostly dry in a few hours.

Neither Ephraim nor Lenora had mentioned Noah, but he knew that the heaviness between them wasn't all due to the weather and work at hand.

She sat across from him during their lunch, fidgeting. At long last, she said, "He wouldn't have come that far every night if something wasn't wrong over there." She stared at her potatoes and drummed her fingers at the side of her plate.

Ephraim turned that over in his mind, the very thought he'd been thinking for days. "Maybe not."

Now that she had spoken, Lenora's speculations turned from a trickle to a flood. "He just didn't seem the kind of boy who would steal, not without reason. You don't know ... they could be without. He might've done it without his pa knowing."

"Hell, Lenora. His pa might've put him up to it." Ephraim spoke sharper than he intended.

Lenora closed her mouth. Her face reddened.

"I'm sorry, I'm sorry." Ephraim reached out for her hand. "I've been worried about it too. Just don't know what to make of it."

She sighed heavily and put her forehead down on their clasped hands.

"What do you want to do?" he asked. "Do you want us to ride over there and check on things?" He stroked her hair with his other hand. Lenora raised her face. Her hazel eyes glinted with little flecks of gold.

"That would be all right, wouldn't it? Just drop by. Neighbors checking on neighbors."

EPHRAIM SADDLED TIP AND CHERRY, Lenora's chestnut mare. He strapped a bag containing a few yams and a loaf of sourdough behind his saddle. They started out north with Tip leading. Ephraim twisted around to see Lenora bundled in a gray woolen coat. She'd wrapped a scarf around her head and neck, covering her face up to her eyes. He admired her for a moment longer, then turned his gaze back to the snowy path.

The Rains place looked even more forlorn by daylight. The shakes on the cabin roof were curled in places, absent in others. The horse pens were in decent shape but Ephraim saw now that the pole shed was missing its front wall because someone had stripped off the planks, presumably for firewood. A few splintered pieces were stacked at the cabin's side wall.

Ephraim waved for Lenora to stay back while he dismounted and approached the cabin. He bumped the door twice with the flat of his gloved hand. After no immediate answer, he called out, "Mr. Rains. It's Ephraim Teller from the south valley. The wife and I ... we thought we'd see how you all are making out in the cold."

He heard the scrape of the bolt being slid open. The door cracked just a few inches and Noah's freckled face appeared. He looked more gaunt than Ephraim remembered.

"Miss Lenora and I been out riding. Figured we'd say howdy. Oh, and she has a loaf of fresh bread for you."

Noah finally said, "We thank you, Mr. Teller. My pa ... he ain't here right now."

"Oh, well....we'll just leave it with you then." Ephraim trudged back to get the bag. *No sign of anybody leaving on foot or horseback. And where's his ma?*

Noah reached for the package without stepping outside, or inviting Ephraim in. "Thank you, sir. Thank you both." He glanced toward Lenora, who was still sitting on the mare. "That Miz Teller's horse?"

Ephraim nodded. "Yep. Calls her Cherry. Reckon you can guess why."

Noah did not respond.

"If you all need anything, be sure to let us know."

"I – we will," said Noah. "Thank you."

Ephraim mounted Tip and he and Lenora headed back. They'd ridden about fifty yards when they heard someone cry out behind them. Ephraim jerked up on the reins.

"Did you hear that?" said Lenora.

"I did." They swung the horses back around.

Noah stood in front of the cabin, coatless, with his arms hanging limply at his sides. The chilling breeze whipped at his hair and faded shirt and pants. He looked the picture of defeat.

Ephraim jabbed his heels into Tip's sides and the horse took off, kicking up chunks of snow. Lenora followed close behind.

When they had dismounted, Noah walked wordlessly into the cabin, leaving the door half open. Ephraim stepped in. Lenora laid her hand on his back as she entered behind him and then closed the door.

There was a modest fire burning but the single room was by no means warm. Two children, a boy and girl, sat on the low hearth, each wrapped in a blanket. The boy, about five, was a younger version of Noah. The girl was only a toddler. She held an empty thread spool between her hands, as if she'd been playing with it for a toy. On the stone hearth between them was a bowl half-filled with something that looked like corn mush.

Noah was sitting on the edge of an unmade bed. A more miserable human Ephraim had never seen. Like a miniature old man, the boy's thin shoulders were slouched and he stared blankly at the floor.

Lenora walked over and sat beside him, motioning for Ephraim to sit down on the other side of the boy. Noah straightened up for a moment, then leaned forward with elbows on his knees, propping his head in his hands. The children watched with eyes wide.

"Ma died toward the end of the summer," he said softly. "She coughed and coughed for a long time, and just wasted away."

"Oh, Noah," said Lenora. "I wish we had known. We should have been more neighborly all along." She unwrapped her scarf and draped it around his shoulders.

Ephraim took a deep breath and let it out. "How about your pa?"

Noah cleared his throat. Ephraim sensed he was holding back tears. "We was rounding up a little herd of mustangs ... last fall. October, maybe. Boxed them up in a draw. Had our eye on a buckskin. Good looking. Pa ran up close and got a rope on him and then a yearling colt got between them. He kicked Pa hard, right in the chest."

He got quiet. Lenora tried to pull him toward her but he resisted. He was intent on finishing the story.

"Pa was hurt bad, I could tell, but he put on like he wasn't. Time we got back home he could barely walk and was spitting up blood. Wouldn't hear of me going for help. He wasn't thinking straight or he would've let me. I should've anyways. I woke up during the night to look after him and he had ... already gone on."

"Son, you didn't know," said Ephraim. "You were just minding your pa, like you were supposed to. There probably wasn't anything could be done for him."

"Reckon not. But I still wished I'd have gone. I buried him myself next morning. When it turned cold, I let what horses we had go so I didn't have to feed them. Turned out to be a bad winter but we been making out all right, mostly. Ain't we, young 'uns?" He opened his arms. The two got up from the hearth and moved shyly into his embrace.

Ephraim was incredulous. *What the boy had gone through. And to take care of the little ones all by himself!*

"Why did you stay here?" Lenora's voice was hardly more than a whisper.

"I was afraid."

"Of what?" she said.

"That if somebody found out we didn't have a ma or pa they'd take us off somewhere … and we'd lose the place. It's all we got left. I can break horses on my own when it gets warm. You don't believe it but I can."

"Oh, I believe it," said Ephraim. "It's not a good job to be doing alone though." He knew he didn't have to explain the dangers of horse handling to Noah.

Lenora reached behind Noah to touch Ephraim's arm. Their eyes met over the trio of blond heads. They had been together long enough to know the other's thoughts. Ephraim nodded.

"Well, Noah Rains. I might have a business proposition for you," said Ephraim. "If you're interested …"

Noah tilted his head. "Interested in what?"

"What do you say the Rainses and the Tellers throw in together? You fellows can stay at our place but we each keep deeds to our own ranches. Unless, of course, you end up buying me out later." Ephraim winked.

Noah's countenance changed from hopelessness to relief to gratitude in the space of ten seconds.

"EVERYBODY HANG ON. We'll have to hustle to get home before dark." Ephraim handed up the two little ones to Lenora. She scooted back in the saddle to fit them in front of her, cloaking them inside her coat like a hen covering chicks. Ephraim saw that her eyes were brimmed with tears.

He got on Tip and pulled up Noah to sit behind him. He held to Ephraim's coat, as if from habit.

But the feel of the boy's clinging hands, and the gentle weight of the small body leaning against his back were very new to Ephraim. His own eyes grew misty. *A blessing to get the first one. And the second and third ones were heaven too.*

"Let's go home, Tip," he said. In single file, they retraced their tracks in the snow.

ABOUT THE AUTHOR

Vonn McKee brings deep storytelling to the western genre, rich with emotion and vivid pictures of a beautiful but unforgiving land and the hardy, spirited people who settled it. She often weaves real-life historical events into her writing, adding realism and intimacy to the characters and storylines.

Vonn broke into the western writing scene in 2014 with The Songbird of Seville, a short story that was chosen as a Spur Award finalist by Western Writers of America. That same year, The Gunfighter's Gift was named a finalist for the Peacemaker Award for short fiction by Western Fictioneers.

She grew up in the Red River Valley of Louisiana, where her mother's family settled in the mid 1800s, and spent summers at the northwestern Minnesota ranch where her father grew up, picking up details about horses, cattle, and agriculture. Inspired by seeing her grandfather stretched out on a sofa reading Zane Grey novels (some of which were passed down to her), she owned a complete ZG set herself by age eighteen. Vonn loved hearing her grandmother relate stories of her childhood spent on the Dakota prairies, which were similar to Laura Ingalls Wilder's accounts in the Little House series of books.

Vonn McKee now calls Tennessee home. She has reviewed books for Roundup and True West magazines and, although her first love is writing short fiction, she is working on a historical novel series.